JOURNEY

TO

EMMAUS

By MaryGrace Dansereau

Journey to Emmaus
Copyright © 2016 by MaryGrace Dansereau
All rights reserved.

All biblical quotes are from the New American Bible
revised edition © 2010, 1991, 1986, 1970 Confraternity of
Christian Doctrine, Inc., Washington DC All Rights
Reserved

Acknowledgements

What does answered prayer look like? What happens when a desperate cry erupts from a despondent heart, flies through the heavens, and pierces the immense and utterly generous heart of God? Such questions wove their way through my heart one sleepless night and I began to wonder what happens *after* we pray. What does God *do*? Images of thunderbolts, wild horses, and sunsets ran through my mind. My quest itself turned into a prayer and this story erupted in my heart in a flash. However, the challenge for me was being patient with its gradual unfolding in time as I wrote and rewrote it so many times. The characters developed and came to life, each one a different aspect of myself, yes, even the 'bad guy', and each one had part of the story to tell.

Throughout the whole process, I have been privileged to have faithful companions travel with me on this writing path and I am grateful. To Charlotte Foster who read my first draft and encouraged me to keep writing. To Erin McKeon, who read it from the perspective of a young person, and was touched. To those in my writing circle, family and friends, who were always available to answer my questions and provide me with thorough and honest critiques for every rewrite and edit: Tommie Lyn, Cecilia Marie Pulliam, and Sylvia Stewart, to my daughter, Teresa Tuttle, and my son, Stephen Dansereau. And to my parents, Mary Anne and Salvatore Ciarmiello, who made every sacrifice to raise me to be the person I am today. Their lives embody a significant truth. Once we embark on a journey, it's not the destination that matters, but the steps that take us there. And thanks be to God, to whom nothing is impossible, who turned this story into a song that remains in my heart as evidence that no prayer goes unanswered.

I dedicate this book to the beautiful students of the Academy of the Holy Names in Albany, New York. You ladies make it a joy to get up in the morning.

And to you, Mom and Dad, because you taught me that …

Emmaus is not so much a place,
as a journey.
We are called by God
to mission, communion, joy, love
… eternity.
Wherever we are when we recognize the call
within
and follow it
… that is Emmaus

CONTENTS

Chapter 1

The Journey Begins

A door opened in the sleepy predawn silence. Not even the birds were awake yet. Matthew felt as if he was moving in a dream. He was reminded of a verse he had heard his grandfather recite often. *'Fear not the darkness where the Cimmerian creature dwells and moon and stars do hide. Stand tall then, my boy, for such must flee the Greater Light.'* He had never experienced darkness so complete. Indeed, he had never had a reason to be up so early. Even now he wouldn't be surprised if he woke and found himself in bed.

He tried to hurry, but the best he could manage was slow motion. *Was he dreaming?* He'd pinch himself if he could, but he was too busy. With one hand he held the door open for his two brothers. His other hand clutched a flashlight.

He took one last look over his shoulder as he closed the door, staring into the darkness for any sign of pursuit, listening for the familiar creak of the floorboards. He knew every stress point. The flashlight shook in his hand, his finger poised over the switch.

He bolted across the screened-in patio, almost flying over the basketball he'd left out the night before. It was against house rules to leave their gear out, but an even greater infraction to be late for dinner. He'd lost his television privileges for the night, but at least he hadn't been sent to his room hungry.

Joseph broke his fall, throwing himself like a wedge in front of Matthew, preventing him from shooting down the patio steps like a rocket.

"Slow down," he whispered. "We're going to make it. Okay?"

"Right, Joe. Got it."

Matthew crawled across the threshold and pushed his backpack underneath the railing into the waiting arms of his younger brother, James. He slipped under the railing and reached up to grab Joseph's backpack. Joseph crept over the threshold and stretched his arm up to lock the door before he slid to the ground.

Once they were crouched low against the house, Matthew whispered, "You left the key in the lock."

"I did that on purpose. They'll think the door is jammed and go around to the front. It'll buy us more time."

"Good thinking."

Joseph led the way across the back of the house, slinking within the protective shadow of the eaves. Matthew took up the rear keeping James sandwiched between them. They crawled along the base of the patio and turned the corner, staying low to the ground until they were past the patio windows.

Matthew squeezed between James and the house, still holding onto James to keep him from stumbling off the stone path. One misstep would be enough to set off the motion detector and flood the backyard with light. He slid from behind James and squatted in front of Joseph, waiting for his signal to take the lead. He felt along the edge of the path for the smooth, shell-shaped rock that let him know they were in the safety zone beyond the boundary of the motion detector. He had carved and placed it there himself.

Excitement began to replace fear as Matthew knelt, poised and ready, for Joseph's signal. Anticipation of victory boosted his confidence. He felt like a horse at the starting gate waiting for the gun to go off. Three taps on his right shoulder and the gate would open. He knew the track better than anyone. He was proud of himself for figuring out the route that led to the woods without tripping the flood lights. It was how he won every game of laser tag he played with his brothers. He could still hear Joseph's laughter when he revealed his laser tag strategy. Little did he know then how that strategy would save them now.

Matthew felt the first tap on his shoulder and took off.

"Matt!" Joseph's strangled whisper reached his ears and he remembered they weren't playing their favorite game. He slowed his pace so his brothers could catch up. They had a narrow margin to follow to remain within the protective darkness between their foster parent's floodlight and their next door neighbor's. Matthew led them down to the Douglas fir then turned a hard left to the woods at the end of the property.

They dropped to the ground as the high beams from a passing car shattered the darkness. Once the car passed, they rose again, continuing to the edge of the property line where they turned and raced toward the safety of the woods.

They were halfway there when Matthew caught the toe of his sneaker in a gopher hole and fell, activating the motion detector, flooding the yard with light. James fell on top of him and his weight and the weight of their backpacks pressed him to the ground. At the same moment, he felt his load lighten and a firm grip pulling him back to the dark zone.

"Joe," he gasped.

"Shhhh! Just lay still till the light goes off."

"It's gonna take four minutes. Mr. Jackson reset the timer … I'm sorry."

"It's okay. Just stay put for now. We'll wait it out."

"But, it's gonna start getting light out."

"We've got plenty of time. Don't worry. Relax, buddy."

Relax. Easier said than done. What an idiot! He could just imagine the police slapping on the handcuffs. They were already facedown.

"Stop beating yourself up, Matt."

"I'm not sayin' anything."

"I can hear you thinking. Shut up."

"Okay, Joe."

Matthew became aware of how comfortable the ground was … cool, soft, damp … and his panic began to subside. He rested his face against the plush grass and allowed it to soak up his sweat. Drowsiness overcame his compulsion to flee … and he called to mind how the events of the previous day came together to form their plan.

****

Was it only yesterday? Matthew and his friend Tony had met in the park to discuss their summer plans. Tony told him about the campground where he used to

4

spend summers with his grandparents. But Matthew was only half-listening as he stood by the lake skipping stones. The fragrance of apple blossoms drifting upon the late spring breeze, carrying the promise of a carefree summer, did nothing to lift his somber mood.

His only plan for the summer was survival. It was all he could think about. He knew his foster mother didn't like him. She didn't like his brothers either, but she didn't like him more. He could tell. He had overheard her on the phone to the agency. She didn't care if he and his brothers were separated. She only wanted them gone.

Joseph became excited when Matthew told him that parts of the campground were deserted and some cabins had fallen into ruin. They had retired early for the evening since Matthew had been sent to his room after supper. He shuffled the cards again and dealt a hand to each brother.

"We could run away, guys; find a place to hide at the campground. It's not too far from here."

"Great idea, Matt. We'll sneak into one of the cabins and fix it up like a secret fort. Shabby on the outside, cozy on the inside. No one'll ever find us."

"But, Joe. I think we should look for a cave. Who's gonna find us in a cave? And besides, when God created Adam and Eve, He put them in a garden, not a house."

In the end, Joseph prevailed. Matthew didn't mind. After all, at seventeen, Joseph was the oldest and a natural-born leader. And he could think under pressure. He had taken care of them after the car crash that killed their parents. *Had it really been more than a year ago?*

They had been moved three times since the accident. Matthew realized their only hope of staying together rested in their older brother's wisdom and patience. He wanted to trust Joseph, but truth be told, he was having a hard time trusting God right now.

Why did his parents have to die? Couldn't they swerve out of the path of that oncoming truck? Couldn't they see it? And why did the drunk driver survive and not his parents? How could God let that happen?

One dreadful moment changed their lives forever and Matthew had been immersed in darkness ever since. And Joseph, wise beyond his years, never lost patience with him through all his fist-pounding grief.

A boring evening turned into a boring night. After what seemed like an eternity, Matthew drifted off to sleep. Shortly after midnight, he felt a nudge on his shoulder.

"Come with me, Matt. I'm hungry." James poked him again.

"You can have the cookies under the bed."

"I already looked. They're gone."

"Can't you wait till morning? I'm tired."

"That's too long, Matt. I'm hungry now. Come on. We'll go fast."

Matthew couldn't say no. He was hungry as well. As they neared the Jackson's bedroom, he heard angry voices coming from inside the room. He put a finger to his lips to warn James to be quiet.

"We're finally getting rid of them, Brian. Gordon told me to have them packed and ready to go by ten o'clock …"

6

Matthew and James looked at each other in stunned silence, all memory of their hunger forgotten. Without saying a word, Matthew took James by the arm and led him back to their room to awaken Joseph.

Joseph sat up, rubbing his eyes. Matthew paced back and forth, the anger rising in his voice. "I knew this was going to happen. I knew it. They're going to separate us. They promised they wouldn't, but they are."

"No they're not. We made a promise to each other. Remember?"

"They don't know that, Joe. And even if they did, they don't care. Didn't you hear me? They're going to pack us up!"

"Get over here and sit down. We need to put our heads together and figure this out."

James threw himself across the bed he shared with Matthew and sobbed.

Joseph put on his slippers and pulled the rocker closer to the bed. He motioned for Matthew to sit in it while he sat on the bed and pulled James up to sit next to him.

"Come on. Let's get to work."

"Don't start with that bossy stuff, Jo ..."

"Sit! Don't make me say it any louder unless you want company."

Matthew froze in his tracks, one foot poised in the air to take his next step, his hands balled into fists. He would have liked to continue his rant. He had a right, but one look in his brother's eyes chilled his rage, for he saw something there he had never seen before. Behind the fierce determination he was so familiar with, he saw fear. Joseph was as scared as he was. He plopped down in the rocker and struggled to hold back his tears.

"They're coming to get us at ten o'clock, Joe."

Joseph folded his arms and closed his eyes. When he opened them, he had that deep, faraway look that signaled quiet authority, like the silence of lightning just before the thunder.

"Let them come. We won't be here. First, let's bow our heads and pray. Remember Mom and Dad's favorite Bible verse – 'where two or three are gathered in Jesus' name, he is in their midst.'"

****

And Jesus, indeed, stood in their midst, radiant and smiling, surrounded by a contingent of the heavenly host. Before the boys uttered a word of prayer, a plan was conceived. The mission was about to begin. Jesus called the angels to gather round as the boys bowed their heads and Joseph led his brothers in prayer.

****

"Abba, we need your help this night. We are desperate, Lord, and only you can help us. Fill us with your Holy Spirit so we can hear you speaking in our hearts. You know our greatest fear. We don't want to be separated. We believe you put us together as a family for a reason and it is your will that we stay together. Please guide and protect us. We know our guardian angels never leave our side. Thank you. Ask Mom, Dad, and Grandpa to stay near us too. We know they are in heaven with you. In Jesus' name we pray."

Matthew and James responded, "Amen."

Before Matthew could open his eyes, he felt two strong hands grip his shoulders firmly. Startled, he looked up into the grinning face of Joseph and relaxed. He also perceived a change in the aura surrounding him though he couldn't describe it. *A sense of calm pervaded the room, dispelling the frenzy of a moment before. Everything appeared to move at a slower pace, and at the same time glistened, as when the sun's warmth burns away the morning mist. Not only did the room seem brighter, he felt a lightness welling up from within and became aware that he was immersed in the light and resonated with it. He wondered if Joseph and James were sharing the same experience but felt no compulsion to ask. He could hear Joseph's voice speaking to him, but sounding as if it was coming from a great distance.*

"Matt? Earth to Matt. Com' on, Matt. Wake up."

He felt a hand clasp each side of his face and move his head … and heard the concern creep into Joseph's voice.

"Matt? Are you okay?"

Matthew shook himself out of his reverie and looked, first at Joseph, then James. Joseph's smile had faded and James looked scared.

"What's going on, guys?"

"You left the planet, bro. Where'd you go?"

"Nowhere. I must have dozed off. I'm okay. But we have work to do."

"It's done, thanks to you."

"Me? Was I talking in my sleep?"

Joseph chuckled. "Earlier this evening, Matt, when you told us about Diamond Lake."

"You mean the cabins? We were just fooling around. Do you really think that will work?"

"It makes perfect sense. Who would think of looking for us there? And in August, we'll be able to carry out our real plan."

Joseph stood, hands on his hips, and looked around the room. "We should pack now so we can be ready to leave before the sun rises. Take only what you can carry in your backpacks. We'll be able to move faster if we're not weighed down. And be quiet. We don't want to wake up the Jacksons. Get dressed now, too, and put your sneakers next to your bed, opened up and ready to slip on as soon as you wake up."

Matthew breathed a sigh of relief. Joseph was again in full command mode. Yet, he wondered. "Why don't we leave right now and really get a head start. I don't think we'll be able to sleep much tonight anyway."

"The Jacksons might still be awake. And, besides, it's too dark now to see where we're going. We need to be well rested so we can cover a lot of ground tomorrow. If you can't sleep, at least get some rest. We'll be leaving early enough to get a good head start. Pack your flashlights. In fact, put them next to your pillows so you'll be ready to grab them. It'll still be dark when we leave."

James squatted and pulled his backpack from under the bed and began filling it. He paused. "What if we oversleep, Joe? How are we going to know when to wake up?"

"Don't worry. I'll set my alarm clock and put it under my pillow. When I feel it vibrate, I'll turn it off and push you both out of bed. Then we'll jump into our sneakers, grab our gear, and make tracks. Mr. and Mrs. Jackson will never hear us. We'll be gone hours before they find out."

Matthew finished packing and climbed back under the covers. He reached over and made sure James was covered and laid back down, pressing his face into the soft coolness of his pillow. He doubted he'd be able to sleep …

****

He felt someone tapping his shoulder and recognized Joseph's whispering voice. "The light's off, Matt. Lead us to the woods; no dancing this time, okay?"

Matthew chuckled. "You missed your calling, Joe. You should've been a comedian. Com' on. Let's go."

Matthew jumped up and ran a straight line into the safety of the woods, his brothers close behind him. They were now beyond the detection of the sensor beam. It was dark, but he knew the path so well he could run it blindfolded. It was a path he trod every day. Their school lay on the other side of the woods, along with the playground and basketball court.

As they emerged, Matthew heard James ask, "What about Nana? Are we going to tell her where we're going?"

11

Joseph shook his head. "Not now, James. That's the first place the police will look for us. If Nana hasn't seen us she'll be surprised we ran away and they won't bother her again."

Matthew agreed. "True. And if we do find a place to stay, we won't be too far from Nana."

Joseph nodded. "If our plan works, everything will be perfect. Once I turn eighteen, I'll adopt you both and then we can be our own family. No one will be able to separate us. We'll move back into our house and take care of Nana like before."

Matthew snickered. "We won't have to call you dad, will we?"

James giggled. "Never happen. As soon as Nana gets better, she'll move in with us. Right, Joe? Then she'll be the boss."

"You got that right, little brother. That would be the best plan."

Matthew laughed. He was again filled with the sense of peace he experienced after their prayer and he felt his confidence return. Maybe they were going to make it after all. *Thank you, Lord! Please help us make this work.*

Chapter 2

Hillcrest

Mary Anne Landolfe hummed a tune as she packaged the remaining breads and pastries of the day. Her favorite end of the day patron was late and she was concerned. She could set her watch by the click of the doorknob, 5:55 sharp. She chuckled every time and her eyes danced at the thought of his arrival.

Tom's wife died five years ago and he still pined for her. She could tell. Oh, he smiled and greeted everyone in his usual friendly style, but only with his mouth now, never his eyes. And he had lost so much weight. His tattered clothes hung low over his bony frame. His wife was the one who had kept him groomed and presentable. He used to tell her the cows didn't care how he looked. Mary Anne heard him say it every time they stepped through the door, always arm in arm. Tom would sneak his hand up to loosen his tie when he thought Maeve wasn't paying attention. And Maeve would reach out with lightning grace and turn him back into a prince.

She chuckled as she called to mind Tom's expression for a tie and could still hear his protest. *'It's a strangulation device, Sweet Pea. A tool of the devil designed to keep a man's eyes focused on his pain and off the Lord. Jesus never wore one of these dang things. Should 'a been one of the commandments.'* Then he would wrap his arms around his bride of fifty years and kiss her while she refused to be distracted. It was their perfectly choreographed dance step.

She glanced up at the clock over the antique juke box … 5:58. *Dear Lord, where is Tom? Please let him be okay. Where can he be?* She looked at the clock again. Three boys were peering through the bakery window. They ducked out of sight when she turned in their direction. She wondered if they were members of the gang that had infiltrated the village over the past year and felt a chill run down her spine. She went back to her work but moved closer to the phone … just in case …

The gang hadn't done anything to break the law so far, but their behavior changed the character of the neighborhood. Dressed all in black, or black and red, and donning bandanas, they hung out on street corners with their music cranked up loud enough to change the rhythm of a beating heart.

The village council was working on having a noise ordinance in place before the end of the school year and she hoped it would happen even sooner. Downtown businesses were losing money. The Book Nook and Candy Lane had already closed up shop and moved to Cricket Hollow. The villagers spent less time in town, shopping and gabbing. Instead of strolling along the boardwalk, catching up on each other's news, they made their purchases and hurried back to their farms. She looked at the stack of boxes she had carried out from the storage room. It wasn't too long ago when there were no leftovers to package. She couldn't wait for the town meeting. The sheriff and his squad were going to unveil their plan to rid the village of the menace.

She tilted her head and peered into the bakery case. This angle afforded her a view of the window without having to look at it directly. She reached into the case to package the doughnuts and saw the boys peering through the window again. She breathed a sigh of relief when she noticed they were not sporting gang attire and chuckled when they didn't duck out of sight again as she reached for another pastry box. They weren't looking at her, but were staring at the doughnuts. Their eyes were wide and their mouths hung open as they pressed their foreheads against the glass.

Mary Anne knew the look well. It was a look that never left her sons' faces during their growing up years, and even now, stretched into adulthood whenever they caught sight of a box of doughnuts. It was a look that turned every hungry child into one of her own. The littlest boy licked his lips and her heart melted. She smiled and waved a hand to get their attention and motioned for them to enter. His eyes grew wider as he grabbed the other two boys' hands and pulled them toward the door.

She greeted them as they entered. "Hello there. Come on in and look around. It's a great time to shop. Everything is half-price."

The tallest boy nodded. "Thank you, Ma'am."

She went back to her work, carefully sliding the shortbread into a pastry box so it wouldn't crumble. Her curiosity kept her attention focused on the boys, and she had to force herself not to stare. *Who were they? They must be new in town.* She would have remembered seeing them before, especially since two of the boys had red hair and sky blue eyes. All three bore enough of a resemblance to be brothers even though the second tallest boy had brown hair and dark eyes. She chuckled to herself. He had a teddy bear look about him that reminded her of her youngest son.

They remained close together, moving in unison, as if held together by invisible cord, keeping the smallest boy between them. She felt a familiar tightness grip her heart and turned away. Tears began to well up from their bottomless spring. The expression on each of their faces told the same story and went beyond hunger. A look of fear was etched that spoke of isolation and lost hope and she prayed silently that Tom wouldn't turn the doorknob now. She had never been able to ignore sadness in a child. What struck her the most, however, was how skinny they were. She wanted to pull them close, and fill their stomachs … and take away their pain.

After a whispered conference, they approached Mary Anne. She put on her friendliest smile and said, "Well, boys, did anything strike your fancy?"

"Yes, Ma'am." The tallest boy nodded at the other two and they pointed at the cookies and doughnuts. "Would you wrap them to go? And will you please refill our water bottles? Boy it sure smells good in here."

Mary Anne smiled. "Why, thank you for noticing. I bake everything fresh here every day." She reached for their water bottles and asked, "Are you boys new in town?"

The change was subtle. The two younger boys edged closer to the taller one. A look of panic flashed between them and they glanced down at the floor. She looked down too, grabbing the cloth she kept handy for wiping away crumbs and wrung it as if it was water-logged. She hoped she hadn't spoiled the magic.

"Yes we are." The tall boy shifted his weight from one foot to the other. "We've just arrived. Our grandfather will be here soon to pick us up from the train station."

He didn't look at her when he spoke and she heard the tremor in his voice. She would like to have asked their names, but she dared not. She had a feeling they were not being truthful. She could tell they were not used to it. It made them look even more out of place.

She filled their bottles with crushed ice and water, put their order in a bag, adding a few more of her own, and placed them on the counter. "The first visit here is always a gift. Welcome to Hillcrest. I hope I have the pleasure of your company again."

Her charm had its desired effect. Smiles lit up their faces as they accepted their treats. After expressing their gratitude, they left the bakery. She reached for another pastry box and glanced up to wave a final goodbye, expecting to see them walk across the front of the bakery on their way back to the train station. Instead she caught of glimpse of them looking over their shoulders and heading in the opposite direction. How strange. She wondered if she would ever see them again …

******

Jake Martini was putting a toolbox in the back of his pickup truck when he noticed a group of boys, dressed in black and sporting bandanas, crossing the street

17

near the woods at the edge of town. They were not blaring their music as they usually did. Nor were they pushing and shoving each other, but were slithering in close formation, like a bobcat on the prowl. Jake knew they were up to no good.

Further up the street, he saw three boys walking together, two tall boys with a smaller boy between them. He could not see their faces, but he noticed they were carrying backpacks. The larger group appeared to be slinking up to the three boys. As the gang closed in, three of them split off and darted into the woods, while the other two sped up the sidewalk.

Jake had observed their strategy many times and knew what was coming. So far, they had been unsuccessful. Their timing was as bad as an alarm clock ringing in the dead of night. He turned to his nephew who was approaching the truck with another toolbox. "Call the sheriff, Rocco. That gang's at it again."

Rocco ran into the shop to make the call while Jake raced up the sidewalk with speed unusual for man his age. He reached the scuffle just in time to pull a big boy off the little one but was hit from behind. He struggled to get up and was struck again. The last thing he heard as blackness closed in was a siren blaring …

****

Matthew and his brothers walked on unaware they were being pursued. They were close to the edge of town now. The trees and foliage were denser, enveloping the boys within welcoming shadows. He felt a rush of excitement as a roadside sign came into view. *Diamond*

Lake Cabin Colony, next right, ½ half mile. The finish line. They were almost there. He turned and held his arm out to fist bump his brothers. James laughed, jumped up, and hit his fist against Matthew's, then spun around and skipped on ahead. The weight of his backpack throwing him off-balance was a comical sight as he exaggerated his steps to remain upright.

Suddenly becoming aware of running footsteps, Matthew called to James to move over and then grabbed Joseph's arm expecting to make room for passing joggers. To his horror, three large boys jumped out of the woods in front of James, while two others closed in from behind. Joseph shoved Matthew toward the woods and darted to grab James, but the gang pushed them to the ground and seized their backpacks. Matthew tried to hold onto his, but Joseph yelled for him to let it go. One of the boys kicked Matthew in the stomach. James was flat against the ground crying, his face pressed against the dirt.

Matthew willed himself to get up, but a sharp blow to the side of his head knocked him off his feet. As he fell to the ground he saw an old man reaching for James and heard his gruff voice yelling, "Break it up!" The last thing he heard as blackness closed in was a siren blaring …

****

Spiraling dizziness engulfed Matthew in waves of nausea. He wasn't sure if the shrill ringing in his ears was coming from inside his head or from the siren on the police car. He forced himself to remain conscious, fighting his way through shades of gray, calling for James. *Was he shouting or did he just think he was?* As he struggled to his feet another wave of nausea brought him back to his knees. He doubled over again, but a firm grip around his waist pulled him to his feet. His legs wobbled beneath him as he was dragged into the woods. He staggered and fell against a tree. "Think fast, Matt." His brother's familiar voice pushed away the remaining fog and brought him back to awareness. A shock of crushed ice and cold water poured over his head washed away the last wave of nausea.

"Sorry about the rude awakening." Joseph handed Matthew his backpack.

"That's okay, Joe. Thanks for the wake up."

James scrambled down from Joseph's back and reached for his backpack. "I'm okay, too. I can run. Let's go."

Joseph led his brothers up a well-worn path, but Matthew resisted. "Isn't the other path better? It's covered over with weeds. No one'll think we went that way."

"You're right, Matt. But the gang went that way and we can't risk meeting up with them. And, besides, this is the way to the cabin colony, so we're still on track. Come on, the sirens are getting closer."

Matthew followed his two brothers. He knew Joseph was right. He also knew it would be getting dark soon and they had to hurry while they could still see where they were going.

The trail branched off in several places as they made their way, but Joseph continued on the main branch. Matthew heard a twig crack in the brush beside them and jumped in panic. He tripped over a trailing vine and sprawled headlong into the brush at the side of the path. An

20

area that glowed with a soft, comforting light caught his attention as he started to climb back to his feet. Joseph grabbed his arm to help him but Matthew pulled him down next to him, pointing to the glow. James squatted next to Matthew and peered through the bushes. The light captivated the three brothers as if to beckon them. They barely dove through the brush as two police officers ran past …

****

Mary Anne heard the sirens and saw the police cars race up the street. She peeked through the window to see what was happening and remembered the boys who had just left the bakery. *Could the police be after them? What if they were hurt?* Across the street, Rocco hurried out of his shop and dashed up the road. She opened the door to get a better view. Near the edge of town, Jake was sitting on the ground and Sheriff Al Benson was bending over him. Panic welled up within her. She finished locking her door and ran to him, crying out, "Jake! Jake! Oh, Jake! What happened! Are you all right?!"

Jake looked up at her and tried to smile, a dazed look in his eyes. "I'm okay, Mare. Don't get yerself in a snit. It'll take more than a tap on my noggin to put me out of the game. Dang thugs!"

He tried to get up, but Sheriff Benson stopped him. "Just rest a minute, Jake. You got more than a tap on your noggin. You don't want to get up too fast now. The paramedics are on their way."

21

Jake rubbed his head. "You shouldn't fuss over me like this. I'll be okay in a minute or two. That little boy might be hurt, though. One of those big oafs was right on top of him. Poor thing couldn't hardly breathe. Where'd he go by the way?"

"They all ran into the woods, Jake. Four of my best men ran in after them. Can you tell me what happened?"

Jake continued to rub his head, staring into the distance. And when he spoke, it was with effort and not his usual vigor. "It all happened so fast, Al. I don't know how much I can tell you. I was getting ready to close up shop for the day when I saw that gang going up the street. They weren't struttin' or listenin' to their loud music like usual. They were just sort of slitherin', like a snake going after its dinner. I could tell they were up to no good. Up ahead, I saw three boys walking together. I knew right away what was going to happen. That's when I yelled to Rocco to call you. Then I ran up here to break up their party. Everything's a blank after that."

At that moment an ambulance arrived and two paramedics got out carrying their black medic bags. While they examined Jake, Rocco and the police officers came out of the woods and approached Sheriff Benson. Officer Pagano handed him a paper bag and reported, "They all disappeared, Sheriff. They just split up and ran in different directions. We did find this bag of baked goods on the ground, though. I suggest we return to the station, come back in unmarked cars and wait. It's going to be getting dark pretty soon. They won't be able to hide in there much longer."

Sheriff Benson thought for a moment and replied, "That sounds like a great idea, Ed, but I don't think we need to waste any more time here. We know who they are and Jake can give us a positive ID. For the next couple of days, patrol on foot in plain clothes. When you see them hanging out again, just bring'em in for questioning. Maybe we'll be able to shake'em up enough to keep this nonsense from going any further."

"Okay, Sheriff. I'll get right on it."

Jake looked up at Officer Pagano, and asked, "Where did that little boy and the two bigger boys who were with him go, Ed? Didn't you see them?"

"I don't know where they went, Jake. They split faster than the gang and vanished. I don't get it. Why would they run when they were the ones who were attacked?"

Mary Anne, who had not left Jake's side, stood up and reached for the bag, "I'll be able to identify them as well. Those three boys just left the bakery. They told me their grandfather was coming to pick them up at the train station, but when they left, they headed this way instead. It surprised me because they didn't seem the troublesome type, but their behavior was suspicious. They were jittery. I thought maybe they were away from home by themselves for the first time. I gave these treats to them as a welcoming gift. I do hope they're all right. They remind me of my own three boys."

Sheriff Benson laughed. "You're such a soft touch, Mare. And, you're right. Those boys weren't the ones causing trouble. But it's obvious they have a reason to run. Our job will be to find out what it is."

Mary Anne turned her attention back to Jake when she heard him turn down a ride to the emergency room at Hillcrest Memorial. "I'm fine," he said. Just a knot on the noggin is all."

Rocco helped his uncle to his feet and held onto him until he was steady. After promising to stay with him through the night and call 911 if any symptoms developed, the paramedics left.

****

Matthew lifted his head, alert to the sounds around him. He had seen the policemen's feet run past them on the path. If they had seen them dive through the bushes, they could be lurking, waiting for them to emerge. He dared not breathe, silently praying to be spared.

The sounds of birds chirping, water gurgling, and breezes rustling through tree branches, reminded Matthew of family camping trips. He sat up and looked around. What he saw took his breath away. He tugged at his brothers and whispered. "You're not going to believe your eyes!" The three boys gazed at the magnificent scene before them.

They found themselves in a small clearing surrounded by tall trees, flowering shrubs, and a thick carpet of velvety green grass just ripe for bare feet. Birds chirped in the trees. Rabbits hopped about on the lush lawn, nibbling on colorful flowers. Squirrels and chipmunks scurried across the grass chasing each other up and down trees and around the bushes. Large, puffy white clouds floated across the vast cerulean sky. The scene was incredibly beautiful and tranquil, an oasis in the middle of the dark woods.

Joseph rose first and led his brothers down to the gurgling brook. They stood at the water's edge awestruck, unaware that their heavenly guard had cast the luminous glow that had attracted them. The angels would enclose and protect them until they were ready to move on.

Matthew was the first to break their silence. "Was that thunder, little brother, or did I just hear your stomach growl?"

James gave his brother a playful shove. "Very funny, bro. I'm hungry! When do we eat?"

Matthew wrapped his arms around James and rubbed his stomach. "Wow, you're right, James. Your stomach's emptier than your head. I'm shocked. And to think, we ate a mere six hours ago."

"Let me spell it out for you, genius. I'm hungry!"

"I think we're safe here for now," Joseph said. "The police already ran by this spot. I'll get the bag from the bakery."

But the bag was nowhere to be found. He returned to his brothers empty-handed. "I can't find the bag. I must have dropped it when we ran into the woods. I'm sorry, guys."

"That's okay. The lady said to come back anytime," James reminded him. "Let's go back and get more."

"We can't go back into town now. I'm sure the police are keeping an eye out for us."

Matthew agreed. "The lady was getting ready to close, anyway. Besides, it will be getting dark soon and we probably should get going. I still have a box of cookies in my backpack we can eat. I'll get them."

James began skipping along the brook gathering stones, while Matthew went to get the cookies. Joseph watched him get ready to skip a stone across the brook. James went through his usual wind-up, then stopped and looked around him, sniffing the air.

"What is it, little brother?"

"I smell apples, Joe." James pointed at the trees and bushes. "Wow, look at all the fruit. Look at all those berries."

Matthew returned with the cookies and stood with his brothers. They gazed on bushes filled with plump berries of all kinds and trees laden with fruit ... bright red apples, golden pears, rich purple plums, and velvety peaches.

"This is incredible," Joseph said. "How can all this fruit be ripe so early in May?"

Matthew's eyes sparkled, and when he spoke, his voice was filled with awe. "There was a scene just like this in a book I read. This must be heaven's feast. Ours is not to reason why. Ours is to just dig in."

James was already plucking strawberries the size of his fist. The fruit melted in their mouths. After eating their fill of the fruits and quenching their thirst from the brook, they rested.

Matthew propped himself up on one elbow. "Maybe we can stay here. I bet we can find a corner to hide."

26

Joseph viewed the surroundings. "It is tempting, Matt, but I think we are too close to town. We didn't run into the woods too far before we stumbled upon this place. And the police are not going to give up."

James laid his head in the crook of his arm and scratched at the ground. Joseph reached over and cupped a hand under his chin. "Don't worry. We're gonna be all right."

Matthew agreed. "You're right, but it is so comfortable here. I still can't believe we got away. We should thank God for helping us and for finding this place. I don't think I've ever been in a more beautiful garden."

"I was just thinking the same thing. This is how I imagine heaven. Maybe it's a sign God heard our prayer."

Joseph pulled James on his lap and held him close. He folded his hands over James' and led their prayer. "Abba, thank you for bringing us to this beautiful garden and for providing us with a delicious feast. We are grateful to you for helping us escape from the police and the gang. We ask you to continue to watch over us and help our plan be successful."

James added, "And bless the lady in the bakery who was so nice to us."

All three boys responded, "Amen."

****

The light radiating from the angels standing round the garden shone with greater splendor. And Jesus was with them, whispering his own 'Amen'

*Joseph, Matthew, and James felt a gentle,
caressing breeze envelop them*

Chapter 3

The Storm

Jake and Rocco finished closing up shop while Mary Anne went to the market to pick up fixings for dinner. Jake was waiting for her when she came out.

"Hop in, Mare. Did you get us anything good?"

"Nice pick-up line, Jake. Should you be driving? You can leave your truck at the shop and ride home in my car."

"I'm okay, Mare. I didn't really get hit all that hard. There's not even a bump anymore. It was more of a shock than anything else and a bit more excitement than I'm used to. No hooligan's gonna keep me down." He smoothed his hair over the spot where the bump had been and added, "by the way, beautiful lady, what's for dinner?"

"Real smooth, Jake. It's your lucky day. I'm going to cook chicken and mashed potatoes. And I have an apple pie from the bakery."

"An offer I can't refuse. If you'd like, I'll go to your place now and fire up the grill for the chicken while you whip up a huge batch of your famous mashed potatoes. I'll bring over ice cream to go with the pie, too. By the way, Rocco took your car to his apartment to get the things he needs to stay overnight with me. Then he'll park it at your place and ride in with me in the morning." Jake knocked on his head. "See, there's nothing wrong with my noggin'."

"At least it doesn't sound hollow. And great idea. I'll look forward to your grilled chicken."

Mary Anne settled back into the cushioned seat of Jake's pick-up and enjoyed the ride home. Jake serenaded her all the way to her cabin.

****

Matthew followed his brothers out of the clearing, continuing the course they had been on when they stumbled into the garden, following it deeper into the woods. Leaving was difficult. They had discovered an oasis but knew they couldn't stay. Nightfall would soon be upon them and the intuition to move on was strong. He knew they didn't have far to go and the path was well marked but strewn with rocks and low-lying branches. It was most likely a common trail used by the cabin residents as a hiking route into town. They walked uphill for most of an hour before James became too tired to walk. Joseph and Matthew took turns carrying him on their backs while the other brother carried all three backpacks. James helped, even then, by holding two flashlights over the shoulders of the brother who was carrying him.

The trail finally ended, opening upon a scene that was a welcome delight. The three brothers cheered and whooped, their raised fists pumping the air.

"We made it, Joe," Matthew said, helping James down from Joseph's back. "This must be the place. I hear a dog barking and I see a cabin across the meadow. There is smoke rising from the chimney. And there's a stream."

"You have eagle eyes, Matt." Joseph squinted, trying to see everything his brother described. "I can just make out the cabin with all the trees around it, and I don't see any smoke rising."

James was looking in the opposite direction, "Look! A deer! Wow! Two deer! A mother deer and her baby are coming out of the woods!"

The three boys crouched down just inside the trees and watched the two deer gracefully stride toward the stream.

Matthew whispered, "I hear water flowing somewhere. There must be a waterfall rushing down from the mountain that feeds the stream. Don't you think this is a great place? And that mountain is huge. We'll have our pick of hundreds of caves."

Joseph chuckled. "Matt, you should have been an eagle or a bear, or some other wild animal. Obviously, God made you to live in the great outdoors."

Matthew turned his attention back to the deer, lost in thought. He watched the doe and fawn drink from the stream and then gracefully stride back into the woods. "I wish we never had to enter another building ever again. Wouldn't that be awesome? Don't forget, big brother, that when God created Adam and Eve, He put them in a garden, not a house. We were meant to live in nature, in wide open spaces ... the great beyond." Then he stood up, and with his arms outstretched, proclaimed, "Verily, verily, I say unto you, roof is a four-letter word!"

Joseph laughed. "Step off the pulpit, Reverend Valente. It's getting dark and we still have to find shelter for the night. Maybe there is a deserted cabin nearby. It appears that we are at the far end of the cabin grounds."

"Or a cave a bear isn't using."

James' eyes grew wide with fear, and Joseph assured him, "Don't worry, little pal. We'll find a place without bears."

James whispered, his voice trembling, "But what about bats, Joe? They come out a night, you know."

Matthew slapped James on the back. "Good thinkin', ole buddy. The caves'll be empty. Let's go find one."

Joseph shook his head and laughed. "Let's just try to find a cabin before it gets too dark."

****

Martha stood at her counter kneading dough and looking out a window of Cabin 33 watching three boys walk across the clearing toward the foot of Mount Gilead. She had been standing there as they emerged from the darkening woods. She watched them jump up and down for joy as they reached their destination and wrestle with playful abandon. And she watched the sky and observed the dark clouds drawing near …

She was ready for the boys but had to approach them at the right time or they'd bolt. The angels were helping by veiling another abandoned cabin set further back in the woods. That cabin was needed for another part of the mission. The angels also inspired the boys to seek shelter near the base of Mount Gilead. Soon they would come upon a dilapidated lean-to. Martha hoped they would

32

decide to lodge there for the night. The weather was also cooperating. It was getting dark fast so the boys would still be nearby when the storm hit. When it did arrive, she hoped panic would not overwhelm them and they would heed the inspiration to follow her.

****

Matthew followed his brothers along the base of the mountain, keeping alert for possible hiding spots. He knew that if the police came looking for them they could hide better in the mountains than in the woods. He became distracted when Joseph pointed ahead. "I see something that looks like a fort behind those trees."

The 'fort' turned out to be a lean-to. It was a wooden structure enclosed on three sides. The roof that covered it slanted downward over the front, which was completely open. It was situated close to the stream and across the footbridge that led to the cabin Matthew detected when they emerged from the woods.

"This will have to do for tonight. It's getting too dark to keep looking," said Joseph. "We can look for something better tomorrow."

"Or more entertaining, right little brother?" Matthew gave James a playful shove.

James shoved him back and then bent down and began gathering pine needles. "We can put these in the fort to make it soft for sleeping."

"Good idea, James. Matt, you help him while I form a trench all around the base in case it rains," Joseph said, as he found the perfect stick for the job.

They were so intent on their chores they did not notice the darkening clouds.

****

Martha was aware of the approaching storm as she sat in her rocker sipping hot tea and watching the boys through the French windows. Her son was right. They were wonderful boys. It would be a pleasure to work with them. And "work" was not quite the right word. This was one mission she felt down deep couldn't fail.

She had driven into town earlier in the day to purchase supplies for a simple meal of soup and bread. As she chopped vegetables and kneaded dough, she thanked Abba for inviting her to be part of this special mission. The anticipation of success filled her with excitement. But it was an excitement tempered with reality. There had been missions that had not succeeded. Plans had gone awry. Inspirations had been ignored as vain imaginings or simply had been unnoticed. Sometimes fear or anger became insurmountable obstacles that prevented people or nations from coming together in peace or reconciliation. In extreme cases, war broke out. There had been times when she could only bow her head and weep as her son had wept over Jerusalem so long ago. At such times, Abba would gently take her to His bosom and hold her, reminding her that the ultimate battle had already been won. Sometimes a mission would have to change to succeed, but down through the generations, there had been many more successes than failures. And failures were only temporary setbacks because, ultimately, Love triumphed. When time reached

34

fulfillment, everything would be accomplished according to Abba's plan. And the rejoicing? It would be without end.

She rose from her musing and walked over to the stove to stir the soup. Two long loaves of French bread had risen to perfection. She gently caressed the smooth surface of the dough and placed them in the preheated oven. Soon the irresistible aromas would waft out of the chimney and windows of the cabin and greet the nostrils of three very hungry boys. She couldn't wait to feed them.

****

Matthew sat with Joseph at the edge of the stream watching the last rays of the sun disappear beneath the horizon. James stood a short distance away skipping stones across the stream. It had been a long and busy day but they enjoyed a sense of accomplishment and were grateful. Their success strengthened their resolve. Their determination to stay together would motivate them to overcome any obstacle. And they believed God was on their side.

James began his wind up routine to skip a stone, but stopped. He turned and came running back to his brothers, exclaiming, "I smell something sooooooo good, like Mom's soup. Boy, am I hungry!"

Matthew laughed. "What a shocker, little brother. I'm hungry, too. How 'bout you, Joe? Maybe we can find some berry bushes."

Joseph shook his head. "It's getting too dark now to search. And we don't know this place well enough.

There are still some cookies and juice in my backpack. Let's have a picnic down by the stream."

Matthew agreed. "And I have rolls and oranges. We can have a feast."

While Joseph went to get the food from their backpacks, Matthew and James spread out a blanket by the stream. After setting out their supper, Joseph led them in grace.

****

A faint rumble of thunder awoke Matthew with a start. He lay still, hardly daring to breathe, alert to the sound of the wind howling through the trees. He wondered if he should awaken his brothers and move to the shelter of the mountain behind them. Lightning lit up the night sky. He counted the seconds between the lightning and the next rumble of thunder … five seconds. The storm was close. They had made the lean-to comfortable, but it was not deep enough to keep them dry. If they hurried, they might still beat the storm.

Matthew gently nudged Joseph awake. "There's a storm coming and it's not far away. I don't think we can stay here."

Joseph listened for a moment. "You're right," he said. "The trees around us are lightning rods. We need to move now. You grab our flashlights. I'll grab James."

As Joseph spoke, lightning lit up the sky. The booming clap of thunder that followed rent the sky, bringing down torrents of rain and hail. The boys dashed from their refuge and raced to the mountain. The wind-driven rain pelted them, soaking them in an instant. James stirred but Joseph comforted him, "It's okay. We're heading to the mountain."

"Put me down, Joe. I can run, too, and then we can get there faster." James tried to sound brave.

But Joseph heard the tremor in his voice and held him tighter. "Just let me hold you for now. You don't have any shoes on. Will you hold a flashlight like you did before?"

Matthew stopped running suddenly and looked behind them. He called to Joseph, "I hear someone calling us. It sounds like a woman's voice."

"You must be imagining it. How can you hear anything in this storm? Come on. We have to hurry."

They started running again. Again, Matthew stopped and looked back. "Someone is calling out to us. I heard my name. And I hear a dog barking."

The boys looked back and saw a small light moving toward them over the footbridge. A dog was barking. They turned to flee, but a woman's voice called to them, melodious over the chaos of the storm, "Boys, you're going the wrong way. Hurry! Joseph, Matthew, James! Come this way!"

The three boys froze in their tracks. They had just been called by name. *Who knew them out here?* Joseph and Matthew looked at each other, not sure what to do. The dog they heard barking ran closer to them, but stopped short, wagging its tail, and looking at them as if to beckon.

Again, the woman urged them. "I will explain. Just follow Moses. Come on. It's okay."

Moses took a few steps toward the footbridge, then turned back to the boys and barked as if urging them to follow.

Joseph nodded at Matthew. "Let's go."

They followed Moses to where the woman was waiting for them, and together they made their way across the footbridge to the cabin. Thunder rumbled, lightning lit up the sky, and the wind howled as the woman and her dog led the way.

Joseph, Matthew, and James stopped at the bottom of the steps to the cabin. The woman turned to them under the porch awning, pulled back the hood of her rain poncho and smiled. "Hi, I'm Martha and my buddy here is Moses. Come in. We'll get dry and warm by the fire, enjoy a bowl of hot soup, and get acquainted. I've been cooking all afternoon. Isn't it wonderful that God sent me three such fine looking young lads to share it with me?"

Matthew held his ground. "But you knew our names."

"That I did, Matthew. I knew your parents. As for the rest, our story will unfold in front of the fire. Now, join me. You've come a long way and must be hungry."

Moses looked up at them, barked, and dashed up the steps. Martha opened the door and stepped in, and Moses followed. Joseph nodded at his two brothers. They followed Martha into the cabin and were immediately greeted with a warm, crackling fire, and the inviting aroma of homemade soup and fresh-baked bread.

Martha showed them to a bedroom where three sets of clothing were laid out on a large four poster bed. She pointed toward the door. "The bathroom is right across the hall. Feel free to shower if you'd like. And leave your wet clothes in the hamper. When you're comfortable join me in front of the fireplace for supper."

Then she left them alone.

Matthew walked around the bed. "It looks like Martha knew we were coming."

"And I feel like I know her," said Joseph, "but I can't quite place her. I'm sure she saw us out there in the field from the window, and the lean-to is just across the footbridge. She must have seen the storm coming and got ready to invite us in."

"She reminds me of Mom," James added, "only older."

Matthew agreed. "And the food smells good. So let's not waste any more time or we'll waste away. Then he spread out his arms, but Joseph dashed over to him and put his hands over his mouth. "This is no time for a pulpit announcement, Reverend."

He pulled Joseph's hands down and whispered, "Verily, verily, I say unto you, food is a four-letter word."

Joseph and James giggled. Sitting by the fire, Martha also giggled.

After showering and changing into dry clothes, they joined Martha in front of the fire and soon were hugging steaming bowls of vegetable soup. On a table in front of them was a basket filled with thick slices of fresh-baked French bread. Moses was asleep, curled up on a rug near the fireplace. Outside, the wind-driven rain and hail pounded against the windows. Lightning lit up the sky and thunder rumbled. Inside the warm cabin, Martha began to tell her story.

"I knew your mother, Rose, from birth. She was a beautiful baby with her curly, red hair and big blue eyes. She grew up right before my eyes into a stunning, young woman. Always singing. Always cheerful. Joseph you look just like her."

Martha stared into the fire as she continued to reminisce.

"I knew your father, Simon, as well. Rose and Simon met in high school after Simon moved to Valley Falls. They were attracted to each other at first glance. After graduation your mother went to State College to get a degree in elementary education and your father joined the Air Force."

"Dad was a hero," said James, swelling with pride. "He won a purple heart in the Middle East War."

Martha smiled at James. "Your dad was a brave man. He became one of the best pilots the Air Force ever had. He and your mom were married as soon as he finished his tour of duty. Matthew, you are the spitting image of your father, and you definitely inherited his sense of humor."

Matthew put his bowl of soup on the table and stood up and took a bow.

Joseph said, "Matt is our own personal preacher. Maybe someday he'll take his show on the road … maybe somewhere way far away from here."

Martha clapped her hands and laughed, then leaned over and cupped her hand under James' chin. "James, you are the perfect blend of both of your parents. Your smile and bright eyes light up a room the same as your Mama's did. And you are strong and brave just like your dad."

She leaned back in her rocker and continued, "I was so sorry to hear about the accident and wondered what became of you boys. I heard you moved in with your grandparents."

Matthew remained silent deferring the floor for Joseph to decide what should be shared. Joseph stared into the fire for a moment before he began.

"You knew our parents well, Martha. Mom loved teaching but quit her job to stay home with us. Dad coached our track teams. And he was a great carpenter. Whatever Mom wanted he made for her. Home was fun. Every Sunday Grandma and Grandpa came over for dinner."

Matthew laughed. "Grandpa was a comedian, too. He never let an opportunity go by."

Joseph chuckled. "Go ahead, Matt. You tell the story about the house. You tell it better than anyone."

Matthew picked up where Joseph left off.

"It's my favorite Grandpa story. Dad used to tell it even better. When our parents got married, Grandpa and Grandma gave them a toaster for a wedding gift and told them that when they came back from their honeymoon there would be something better than sliced bread to go with it. They had bought one of the new townhouses and worked hard to move out of their house and have it ready for Mom and Dad. When they came back from their honeymoon, Grandpa picked them up from the airport. They thought they were getting a ride to their apartment, but Grandpa knew the owner of the apartment building and was able to cancel the lease. He told them Grandma had dinner ready back at the house. It was a bright, sunny day and all the neighbors were out on their porches. Mom was waving at everyone as she rode up the street."

Matthew sat up straighter, rested his elbow in the arm of the rocker and imitated the 'Queen's wave'."

Martha clapped her hands with delight. "Yes, your Mama and Grandpa had the same sense of humor. I can still see her trademark greeting."

"Grandpa parked the car in the driveway and they climbed up the porch steps. There was a brown envelope sticking out of the mailbox. Grandpa pulled it out, read it, and told Dad that it looked like he had important mail. When Dad opened the envelope all the color drained from his face. In his hands, he was holdings the deed to the house in the name of Mr. and Mrs. Simon Valente. Grandpa said it was the only time he ever saw Dad cry. Then Grandpa picked Dad up and carried him over the threshold."

Martha smacked her hands down on her lap and laughed. "I didn't have to be there to imagine that scene. It was their philosophy on life … humor first, last, and always."

Joseph said, "There's even more. Fill us in, Matt."

Matthew's brown eyes sparkled. "Dad ran back outside, swooped up Mom and carried her over the threshold. Then Grandpa picked Grandma up and carried her outside the threshold. The neighbors had gathered in front of the house. Then Joe and Emma Perkins handed Mom an envelope and told her it was more important mail.

Mom opened it to find a gift certificate from the neighborhood for the Royal Furniture Depot. Afterward, everyone gathered in the Perkin's backyard for a picnic. Mom said it was like another wedding reception."

Martha laughed and clapped her hands again. "What a wonderful story! Thank you for sharing it, Matthew. I lost touch with your parents after the wedding. I moved out here intending to keep in touch but started teaching again. Your parents became busy raising you boys, and they did a wonderful job, I might add."

"Thank you, Martha." Joseph picked up the story. "Life was great. As we got older, Mom decided to get back into teaching so she could help send us to good colleges. Mom and Dad were on their way home from an interview when they were hit head-on by a drunk driver. Grandpa and Grandma moved back in with us and sold their townhouse. Our pastor helped too. We had dinner together every Friday."

"Father Paul made the best ice cream sundaes," James added.

"Yes he did," said Joseph. "He helped us through a very difficult time. Then Grandma had a stroke and ended up at the Valley Falls Nursing Center. We went every day after school and did our homework with her. She wouldn't leave until she was satisfied that we knew our work."

"Her doctor said that were helping her get better faster," interrupted Matthew, "because we kept her brain working."

"Especially you," said Joseph, chuckling. "Your spelling always had her staring at the ceiling."

Martha chimed in, "I hear you're good at four-letter words, though."

Joseph groaned and shook his head. "It doesn't take much to encourage him, Martha."

Matthew was already on his feet, taking a bow.

Joseph leaned forward, his elbows resting on his knees, his face cupped in his hands, and stared into the fire. "Grandma was still recuperating when Grandpa had a heart attack and died. We were stunned, but we didn't blame God. Mom and Dad taught us that God doesn't send bad things, but it did seem like a dark cloud was following us around. We were placed in a foster home while the state tried to find a family who'd be willing to take the three of us. And we wanted to stay in Valley Falls so we could be near Grandma. We had to move three times while they searched, but no one was able to take us together. Boys are a big deal, you know, especially since Matt and I are teenagers. Then, last night, we overheard a phone call. We were going to be separated. A friend of ours told us about this place and here we are. We have our own plan, Martha, and I know we can make it work."

James looked pleadingly at Martha, "Please don't tell anyone where we are."

Martha looked at the boys and smiled. "Put your minds and hearts at rest. You boys are safe here. But you must be careful because the authorities will be looking for you. I'm sure you have a great plan, but I don't think others will see it the same way you do. They will probably insist on their own plan. But right now, however, your mission of the highest priority, if you choose to accept it, is to scoop yourselves out three heaping bowls of ice cream while I wash the dishes."

After they had finished their ice cream, the boys help Martha finish cleaning up, and then she showed them to two bedrooms she had prepared for them. "Make yourselves comfortable. This one used to be my son, Sam's room. I read many a bedtime story in here, sitting in that rocker, while he tried to keep his eyes open to hear the end. I finished most of those stories in front of the fireplace while he ate his breakfast. He never outgrew them, either. His bed is big enough for all three of you if you want to camp together. So jump into your pajamas and come back to the fire and we'll pray."

****

After they finished their prayer, Martha tucked them in and kissed them on their foreheads ... just as she had done for her son so long ago.

Chapter 4

The Gift

Mary Anne shivered against the chill morning air. The storm clouds that came during the night stayed to greet the dawn. She fumbled for the key in her pocket and shivered again, pulling her coat more tightly about her. The sun was losing its battle with the clouds, the darkness a foreboding presence that swallowed her hand as she struggled to unlock the door. She couldn't get inside fast enough.

There was another reason for her haste. Tingles of anticipation ran up her spine chasing away the chill of a moment ago. Her daughter, Teresa, would be arriving shortly with her two daughters, Jessica and Bernadette. They had been away the past three weeks and she missed them dearly. She couldn't wait to catch up with them.

She sang to herself as she set the coffee to brew and put the first tray of cinnamon rolls into the oven. These were her favorite kind of days. Everything moved at a slower pace. Her patrons stayed around longer to visit with each other. The grayness of the day was like a natural sedative to rejuvenate the soul, a respite from their busy lives. She hoped the gang would not show up and ruin everything. Glancing up from her work, she espied Jake and Rocco pulling into their service station across the street in Jake's blue pickup. They were up early especially considering what they had been through the day before. Instead of going into their shop, however, they headed toward the bakery. She grinned and her eyes twinkled. The aroma of fresh-brewed coffee and cinnamon rolls must already be carving a path through the gloomy early morning air. They opened the door of the bakery and greeted her.

"Mornin', Mare. You're a jolly sight for sore eyes this fine mornin'. I'm glad we didn't hafta' wait for breakfast. Would'a been tough."

"Good morning. Pour yourselves some coffee and pull up a booth. The rolls will be ready in a few minutes. How's your head, Jake? I'm surprised you're up so early after yesterday. You're not usually open on Sunday."

"We're not open for business, Mare. We just have to get a head start on this week's work or we'll get buried. I think half the town wants their cars serviced for Memorial Day. If they're all goin' away like I heard, this will turn into a ghost town for a couple 'a days."

He added, with a sparkle in his eyes, "Save me a seat next to you in church. I'll be finished in plenty a time. And I'm fine. Dinner was great last night, by the way. Thanks for a wonderful evenin'. We'll have to do that again real soon."

Rocco carried two steaming mugs of coffee over to a booth, as Mary Anne took a tray of cinnamon rolls out of the oven. The door chimed again. Sheriff Benson walked in, closed his eyes and inhaled deeply. "The perfect start to a dreary day. I could smell my delicious breakfast way down the block. So I just had to follow my nose."

"Nice to see you, Al. I'm glad your nose is so smart. And your timing is perfect as well."

Mary Anne put some cinnamon rolls on a plate and carried them over to Jake and Rocco. Sheriff Benson poured himself some coffee and joined them.

As she was returning to the kitchen with an empty tray, she heard the door chime announce another arrival. She set the tray in the sink, wiped her hands on a damp towel, and hurried back out front to greet her guests. Father Luke Powers and his twin, Sister Madeleine, and Deacon John Salerno entered and placed their umbrellas in the stand. Father Luke tipped his hat toward Mary Anne. "Top of the mornin' to you, my lady. The lights and delicious aroma coming from this place are the perfect welcome on this gloomy morning. It feels like we're going to get another downpour any minute. It'll be a delight to be stuck here. Maddie, John, and I decided to move our meeting here real close to your cinnamon rolls. Hope you don't mind."

Mary Anne put three more coffee mugs on the counter. "Sounds like you made a wise decision. Pour yourselves some coffee and start your meeting and I'll pull the cinnamon rolls up close." She sang as she filled another plate and carried it over to their table. "I'm surprised you're having a meeting before Mass."

Sister Madeleine chuckled. "We're going on a picnic today and Luke and John can't stop whining about it. Something about needing the sun." She slapped her hand down on the table and laughed even harder.

John choked on his coffee. Father Luke smacked him on the back and came to their defense. "Today's the day of our Annual Youth Rally and Picnic. We're planning to meet up at Diamond Lake if the weather

49

clears up. But if it doesn't we'll have to gather at the Parish Center instead. Sooommme people, however … and I'm not mentioning any names …" He turned and stared hard at his sister, "are convinced it's going to clear up. Maddie, you could find the sun in a closet."

Sister Madeleine grinned back at her brother. "Wouldn't have to, Luke, because it would be right here in my back pocket. Remember to pack your sunglasses; we'll be up at the lake. I listened to a weather forecast and it's predicted to clear up. Never fret. The gloom will pass."

Father Luke put his arm around his twin and held her close. "That's why you're my favorite sister, Maddie. You're such an optimist, always looking for the rainbow before the storm passes. Well, one thing's for sure. With you around, it'll be sunny and warm, even if we do end up at the Parish Center. The kids love being …"

"My dear brother, I'm your only sister. Good thing we love …"

They heard the motorcycles before they saw them.

"That's some thunder," exclaimed Father Luke, turning toward the windows.

But John jumped up and rushed to the door. "It's worse than thunder." The dark complexion of his Native Indian heritage deepened.

"What could be worse than thunder on the day of our youth picnic?"

"Motorcycles," said John, his voice edged with suppressed rage. "It's the Jaguars. And they're here just in time to ruin the rally, worse than any storm."

He reached for the doorknob, but Sheriff Benson called to him. "Hold on, John. If you try to chase them now, they'll get away. I'll call for a couple of patrol cars to follow them and find out what they're up to. Jake, Rocco, see if you can recognize anyone from yesterday. I realize it'll be like trying to identify a shadow in a cornfield, but check anyway."

Jake and Rocco joined John at the door while Al called for backup. Father Luke, Sister Madeleine, and Mary Anne joined them as well. They stood there and watched the motorcycles pass by. It had started raining again …

****

Matthew woke to the sound of rain pattering on the roof and the aroma of pancakes sizzling on the griddle. Soft footsteps padded up the hallway. Martha gently rapped on the door and entered. She caught Matthew's eye and padded around to his side of the bed. She leaned over and whispered, "Time to get up, sleepyhead. Wake your brothers and come to the table for breakfast. We have a busy day ahead and must plan it well."

She patted his head and left the room. Matthew yawned and stretched. He wished the night's respite could last a bit longer. *Hadn't they just curled up beneath the covers?* He had no clue what time it was. It was hard to tell if it was midnight or if the clouds were doing a great job masking the dawn. He was comfortable and snuggled down a few moments longer listening to the sound of the rain and began to drift off, but Joseph nudged him. 'Martha says we need to get moving. Breakfast is ready."

Matthew stretched himself awake. "It does smell good." He propped himself up on one elbow, listening. "It's still raining. Maybe Martha will let us stay. I bet we can find a hiding place here. Cabins like these sometimes have a door hidden in the wood paneling."

"If there is, Martha probably knows about it and we don't know her well enough. Let's get dressed and pray for guidance."

"And eat," said James, stretching and sitting up between his two brothers, "those pancakes smell great, and I'm hungry."

"Big surprise," laughed Matthew, ruffling James' hair.

After washing and dressing, the boys gathered to pray. As was their custom, Matthew and James waited for Joseph to lead. "Abba, thank you for keeping us safe through the night and for Martha. Please bless her for her kindness to us. She reminds me of Mom, Lord. I hope she is as good as she seems. Please guide us through this day. We pray in Jesus' name."

Matthew and James responded, "Amen."

James looked up at his brothers, his eyes sparkling. "I like Martha. You're right, Joe. She does remind me of Mom."

Matthew walked over to a window and watched the rain cascade down the panes. "I agree, but we need our own backup plan, just in case. She could be a hypocrite, you know."

James opened his eyes wide and whispered, "Shhhhh! Martha might hear you!"

******

Standing in front of the fireplace, Martha chuckled ... Matthew surely had inherited his father's sense of humor, and he never let an opportunity escape.

******

The aroma of their breakfast hung in the air. The boys helped Martha clean up and then gathered in front of the fireplace. It was only their third time, yet Matthew felt like it was something they had done all their lives. Martha sat in her rocker with a Bible on her lap. Moses lay on the floor next to her with his head resting on his front paws. James claimed the child-sized rocker next to Martha and Joseph and Matthew plopped themselves in rockers similar to Martha's. Each wooden rocking chair was covered with plush cushions and draped with a colorful afghan. Matthew and James covered themselves and sank back into the soft cushions. James closed his eyes, but Matthew remained alert, gazing into the fire. He wished he could give himself over to their tranquil surroundings. It was tempting, but he had to remain vigilant. And he noticed that Joseph was doing the same.

Outside, the darkness persisted. It had started raining again. Wind howled through the trees. Rain slammed against the roof and windows. The cozy glow emanating from the fireplace lulled the boys to restful slumber. James snuggled against the cushions of his rocker and fell asleep. Matthew inhaled the aroma of the pancakes and fresh strawberries they had just enjoyed. He watched

Joseph's eyelids grow heavy until he, too, succumbed to the moment. He prayed silently that they wouldn't have to run …

****

A multitude of the heavenly host filled the room deepening their sense of peacefulness. Matthew felt his defenses weaken as drowsiness coaxed him away from his watch. Their guardian angels took up stations beside each of them. He felt a light breeze caress his face, his own angel's kiss. Overcome with a feeling of tranquility, he covered himself with an afghan and rested his head against the soft cushion of his rocker. Everything felt perfect ... just as it had been before the accident ...

And Abba was with them as at the beginning when He spoke and His Word went forth over the abyss ... Breathing Life ... Infusing Hope ... Instilling Love. It was a pivotal moment in the mission. A beam of Light would be sent through Martha, a symphony to pierce the darkness and the darkness could not overcome it. Without her, the mission would fail, and the boys would keep running ... and the world would never know what it had missed.

****

Martha smiled to herself, allowing the moment to continue, wishing it could last. The boys needed to be sufficiently relaxed so they could receive the message in their hearts and respond. There was a delicate balance to be discerned between the trust that was essential and their readiness to bolt. Joseph stretched himself awake and rubbed his eyes. Martha sensed the ripeness of the moment and picked up her Bible. Bookmarks were sticking out from several places. The title was barely visible in the fragments of gold lettering remaining on its cover. Its tattered and frayed edges proclaimed the love of its reader. Martha knew this unspoken message would reach the hearts of the boys and deepen their trust.

The creaking of Joseph's rocker woke Matthew and James. She had their attention as she opened the Bible to one of the bookmarked pages. "I prayed for you boys last night and I believe God brought you here for a reason." Her soothing voice gently coaxed them to wakefulness. "Your courage and determination are the same qualities that Jesus looked for in his disciples. They took a risk and faced ridicule, even death, to remain faithful to him."

Matthew chuckled. "Jesus also lost many of his followers. Every time he said something they didn't like, they ran away." He laughed again and added, "One man even ran away naked on the night Jesus was arrested."

Joseph groaned. Martha giggled. "I can see that you are indeed a biblical scholar, Reverend Valente."

Matthew stood up and took a bow, then settled himself back into his rocker. Martha continued, "And you are right, Matthew. Run scared, they did. But know that fear is not the absence of valor. In fact, it is exactly where courage swoops in and propels us to action. Heroes are those special souls who, though terrified, face their fears, and don't give up until they reach their goal. Jesus' true followers came back and carried his message to the entire known world. They faced imprisonment and death.

Remember, Jesus also hid himself from time to time because his hour had not yet come, and still he fulfilled his mission. That is the real definition of 'running away' for brave people – their hour has not yet come. You boys are on such a journey."

Joseph sat forward and stared into the fire. His inner struggle visible on his tight knit brow as he tried to grasp the idea she had just shared. He turned to her and asked, "How does running away from home make us brave? We are on a mission but we are not in danger of death like the apostles were. We just don't want to be separated."

Martha reached over and put a comforting hand on his shoulder. "Your separation would be a kind of death. God put you together as a family and your desire to stay together is noble. You are witnessing to God's love by the love you share for each other. The agency that exists to help you has a job to do and they have their own solution which conflicts with yours. They are satisfied with a speedy resolution because they are overwhelmed with the number of cases they have to handle. Let me ask you a question. Think about it for a few moments before you answer. Are you running away from or toward home?"

Joseph turned his gaze back to the crackling fire. The rain had decreased in intensity and its gentle pattering lulled him back to restful thought. Martha put her Bible down on her lap and laid her head back against the cushion of her rocker. She closed her eyes, gently rocking her chair.

After a while, she picked up her Bible again, opened it to the fourteenth chapter of John's Gospel, and read, "Do not let your hearts be troubled. You have faith in God; have faith also in me. In my Father's house there are many dwelling places. If it were not, would I have told you that I am going to prepare a place for you? And if I go and prepare a place for you, I will come back again and take you to myself, so that where I am you also may be." She closed the page and sat back. "I'm sure that you've heard this passage many times."

James' eye grew wide with delight. "It was Mom and Dad's favorite. Father Paul read it at their funeral. He read it at Grandpa's too. He said that dwelling places are for people who are alive so we know that when we go home to God we are alive. Mom, Dad, and Grandpa are not dead but living with God forever in heaven."

"Father Paul is right. And that is what usually comes to mind when we hear or read this passage. But, last night, as I prayed for you boys, I prayed over this reading, and a new way of seeing it opened up to me. I came to understand that home is more who we are than where we are. Does that make sense?"

The three boys looked at her with furrowed brows. "I'm not sure I follow you, Martha." Joseph leaned forward in his rocker, his elbows resting on his knees, his face cupped in his hands. He gazed at her intently.

"It is a difficult concept but think of it like this. Have you considered that your strong desire to be together is also God's desire for you? What ... or Who ... is the source of your desire? Settle back for a moment and let's listen again."

The boys leaned back in their rockers, closed their eyes, and listened as Martha reread the passage. She closed the Bible, sat back, and waited, giving time for the words to sink in. Then she asked, "What phrase stuck out the most for you?"

Joseph sat forward and gazed into the fire, his eyes glistening. He replied, "You know, Martha? This time it's different. I always focused on Jesus preparing a place for us, but this time, both times you read it, what I noticed most was that Jesus promised to come back to take us with him so we could be together." A tear formed at the corner of his eye and rolled down his cheek. "It's about unity, Martha. I do believe that God put us together for a purpose. I feel it deep inside."

Martha clapped her hands for joy. "You hit the bull's-eye, my friend. It's all about unity, first with God, and then through God, with each other. Remember the great prayer of unity Jesus prayed that all believers may be one with the Father just as Jesus was and always had been one with the Father. The dwelling place God prepares is within us, our hearts where He can rest his head. We are home wherever we are, in this life and in eternity, as long as we keep united with God. Say this phrase within yourself and let it sink in: 'I Am Home.' Can you hear that home is more about being than location? Its foundation is relationship. God draws us ever closer into a deeper and stronger friendship. So I ask you again. Are you running away from or toward home?"

The message hit its mark. Joseph responded without hesitation. "We are home. We are home, Martha, and God is with us. And it's our mission to find a way to be together."

Matthew folded his arms across his chest and huffed. "If the agency has its way we will be separated. Our mission then will be to find our way back to each other. I bet the police are already out there looking for us, especially after our narrow escape yesterday. We need to find a good place to hide."

"You are right, Matthew, about finding a good place to hide. The police will certainly be looking for you. The most important thing for you to understand now is to remain calm and trust in God. It will be a challenge. You will be tempted to panic and then the outcome will not be good. My son, Sam, can help. He knows these grounds and the mountains around us intimately and has a place special to him on Mount Gilead, the mountain behind us, where he spent untold hours praying and discerning God's will for his life."

The boys turned to each other, their panic visible in their expressions. Martha noticed. "You have nothing to fear. I am certain God sent you to me for a reason. And Sam agrees."

Headlights shone through the windows as a jeep turned up the driveway. Moses woke and bolted to the door, barking and pawing excitedly. James leaped up and darted over to Joseph, a terrified expression on his face. Joseph and Matthew flew out of their rockers, grabbed James, and bolted to the back door. Martha stood up and called to them in the same calming voice she used to get their attention during the storm, "It's okay! It's only Sam, not the police. Come back to the fire. Sam's okay. He's here to help."

Moses darted over to the boys and nestled against them as if trying to ease their panic until Sam opened the door. Crossing the room in one mighty leap, Moses jumped all over Sam, barking and covering him with slobbery kisses. Sam's booming laughter rivaled the thunder of the night before. He grabbed Moses in a huge bear hug then dove to the floor, rolling and wrestling, barking and laughing. Sam came up on his hands and knees, nose to nose with Moses, both of them panting and barking. Joseph, Matthew, and James forgot their panic and doubled over with laughter.

Then Sam grabbed Moses' face, kissed him, and said, "Hold the moment, dear buddy, while I pay proper respect to the fourth commandment." Sam jumped up and scooped up Martha, who made a futile attempt to escape. A gentle, "oh, dear" blew through her lips as Sam lifted her up in his arms, and whirled her around, singing, "Hhhelllllooooo, Captain Mommeeeeeee." Then he tenderly put her down and walked over to the boys.

Sam's strategy worked. The anxiety and panic vanished from the boys' faces. Matthew bent down and whispered to James, "Relax. Bad guys don't whirl their moms around the room."

The angels were laughing, too. Though they were part of every mission, they never knew what kind of entrance the Son would make.

Sam walked over to them and shook their hands, "Hi, I'm Sam. It is nice to meet you, Joseph the third parent. Matthew, or should I say, Reverend Valente. And James the Great. When I called to chat with Mom last night, she told me all about her three handsome guests, and

I just had to meet you for myself. Let's sit by the fire and get better acquainted."

Martha said, "Joseph, Matthew, you two sit with Sam. James, will you help me prepare another round of hot cocoa?"

After a reassuring nod from Joseph, James skipped over to Martha, as Joseph and Matthew followed Sam to the fireplace and reclaimed their rockers. Sam sat cross-legged on the floor near the fire. Martha called to him, "Sit in my rocker, Sam."

"I'm comfortable here, Mom. I'll dry off faster close to this beautiful fire, and these fine boys here will be more comfortable if they realize that they can get away from me faster than I can get back on my feet. If they feel the need, that is. I pray that you boys understand that won't be necessary. I'm here to help."

Martha chuckled as she reached for the kettle. James set five mugs on the table and began to scoop hot cocoa mix into each one. Martha hummed a tune as she inwardly recalled a verse from the thirtieth chapter of the book of Isaiah: 'The Lord will give you bread in adversity and water in affliction. No longer will your Teacher hide himself, but with your own eyes you shall see your Teacher. And your ears shall hear a word behind you: 'this is the way; walk in it,' when you would turn to the right or the left."

****

Logan, Gangster, and Scar rode their motorcycles up Main Street through town toward the

Diamond Lake Cabin Colony. Their destination was Cabin 34 where three new recruits were waiting for them, eager to become members of the Jaguars. And Logan was just as eager for them to join. As the new high chief of the local branch of the Jaguars, he wanted his group to expand rapidly to attract the attention of the home branch down state. They were well on their way to becoming a national organization, and Logan could already see himself in the president's seat.

The three new recruits were troublesome, however. They were too impatient to prove their bravado. And they were making a nuisance of themselves in town. Already sporting the black bandanas that were only permissible after they were inducted, they were much too visible and raucous. But that wasn't the worst of it. The biggest problem with these recruits was that they wanted to drop out of school and move in with the home branch. That kind of behavior was unacceptable to the Jaguars and would cost Logan his dream.

Logan had been hoping to establish an invisible stronghold for the Jaguars in the quiet hamlet of Hillcrest. His research of the area had shown Hillcrest to be a village of longstanding religious families and simple living. Farming and small businesses were their main occupations. It was the perfect place for the Jaguars to lay low whenever it became necessary to hide from the authorities and the last place anyone would think to look for them, especially since their headquarters was so far down state. And it would also be the perfect place to hide their money.

Logan, Gangster, and Scar proceeded up Main Avenue and turned right onto Jefferson Street, entering the cabin colony by the rear entrance. It had started raining hard again and was so dark that the headlights from their motorcycles only reflected back a blinding glare off the driving rain. But they had been this way many times over the past year and could now find their way blindfolded.

****

Nick heard the distant rumble of the approaching motorcycles. He ran to the door and hurled it open. "They're here," he informed his buddies.

Frank and Tony were right behind him.

Tony said, "Are you sure it's them? It's raining pretty hard, you know. Could'a been thunder."

Nick replied, "I know motorcycles when I hear them. They're finally here. We've been waiting long enough."

They crossed the doorway but waited under the protective eave. Nick glanced back at his brother who was seated on a sofa watching a cartoon.

Six-year-old Rick remained inside the cabin. A car accident had almost taken his life two years before and had left him in a coma for three months. When he woke, the doctors discovered that he had no feeling in his legs. Since no medical reason could explain the paralysis, there was still hope that he would recover, but that was more than a year ago, and hope was fading faster than a sunset in midwinter.

Sixteen-year-old Nick, uninjured in the accident, never left his brother's bedside. He prayed harder than ever before for his brother to awaken. His vigil gave him time to reflect on all the times he had been cruel to him. He had become proficient in finding ways to evade him so he wouldn't have to let him tagalong everywhere he went, always jealous that his friends seemed to like him better. Nick had always been socially clumsy, while Rick, on the other hand, was a natural. He could have a fan club everywhere he went but remained disinterested. He only wanted to be with Nick…all the time. It drove Nick crazy. The accident changed all that, however. Nick prayed. And, when no one was around, Nick cried. *How could God let this happen?* Loyal and cheerful, Rick never took offense for anything Nick did to him. Nick felt helpless. The only thing he could do for Rick was pray, and it didn't seem to help. He despaired that Rick would ever awaken. When he did, however, they became inseparable.

As the motorcycles turned up the driveway, Nick ran down the porch steps and darted to open the garage door. Frank and Tony dashed in right behind him. The three bikers rode into the garage, removed their rain gear, and led the way back into the cabin. Logan scowled at Nick when he saw Rick. "I told you to leave him home this time. We have private business to conduct and I can't risk him overhearing anything."

Nick replied, "He was dressed and ready to go when I woke up, Logan. He won't be any trouble. He'll just sit here and watch the tube."

Logan said, "He's less trouble than you three so far. What were you guys thinking yesterday, jumping those boys? Now the police are watching you. And you shouldn't be wearing those bandanas yet, either. Stuff like that won't get you into the Jaguars."

64

Frank jumped in, "We could tell they were new in town. Who were they gonna tell?"

Logan retorted, "What do you mean, 'who were they gonna tell'! The real question here is what was the point? Was there a reason for your madness? If you land yourself in jail, the Jaguars will never accept you. None of us has a record."

Nick answered, "It won't happen again, Logan. We've been laying low ever since. We're not even hanging around in town anymore."

Logan said, "Keep it that way and lose the bandanas. They make you look like thugs. Now follow me."

Tony, Frank and Nick followed Logan, Gangster and Scar over to a table away from Rick where they could speak without being overheard. Seated around the table Logan began their meeting, "As you know, today is the Annual Youth Rally right here at Diamond Lake. You three should attend and help out where you can. Keep your eyes open for any possible recruits. And don't get yourselves into any more trouble. If the police corner you, just apologize. One more thing, finish out the school year. The Jaguars don't take dropouts. This is your last warning."

******

Even though Logan kept his voice low, Rick heard every word. Rick could hear things no one else could hear, such as snowflakes falling on a cold winter's night, flowers opening their petals to the caressing warmth of the sun's awakening, stars twinkling in the heavens in the dark of night. And it was more that he became aware of their movement than it was audible, like witnessing a dance. But whatever it was, his unique ability to hear was a gift from the lady with the beautiful voice who had kept him company in his dreams after the accident. He had never seen her, just listened to her melodious and caressing voice assure him that everything was all right, telling him to rest so he could heal, singing to him. And he could still feel her arms around him as she gathered him into her warm embrace.

Eventually she had given him a choice. He could transition to the eternal realm where she dwelt with God. Or, if he thought he could wait, accept a special task that could only be accomplished through him. His brother Nick was heading down a dangerous path that appeared glamorous on the surface but was deceptive. It was a path that would eventually lead to death. Nick's role in the mission could save his brother's life.

Rick had always looked up to Nick. He admired everything about him and wanted to imitate everything he did. He even dressed like him and followed him everywhere. Nick tried to be elusive, but it never worked. Rick always found him in time. The idea of leaving with the lady was enticing. He was happier than he had ever been in his life, if that was even possible. He was a naturally cheerful child, grateful to be alive. But his brother needed him and the lady assured Rick that she would remain with him. She had bestowed on him his unique ability to help him in his mission. His gift of hearing was both powerful and subtle. He was not bombarded with noise but he could hear anything he focused his mind on, such as the conversation going on at the other end of the room. He could have been outside, or even at home, and still heard every word. The gift also permitted Rick to listen to his heart better, where the lady would continue to guide him. The gift and the mission, however, were a secret between Rick and the lady. *Who else would understand?*

******

After a few last minute instructions, Logan, Gangster, and Scar rose to leave. Tony walked them to the door. Nick turned off the television and lifted his brother from the sofa, while Frank turned off the lights. It was still raining as Nick watched the motorcycles ride off into the darkness. He secretly hoped the rain would continue all day and the Youth Rally would be cancelled. He wasn't looking forward to evading the police while taking care of Rick. And there was no way he was going to leave Rick behind. "Funny how the tables were turned," he mused. "Now he was the one pursuing Rick." The boys put on their rain gear, got on their bikes, and rode home, leaving by the back road.

******

Martha watched them leave, knowing they were part of the mission. Her son was already speaking to them in their hearts. It was up to the boys to listen, but they were also in a very fragile state. Martha felt the familiar sorrow in her heart that accompanied knowing not all of them would heed the call and she grieved for them already. But she also knew that Jesus would call them again, and again, until they did answer. He would not allow anyone whom the Father gave Him be lost. And she would be there to help.

Tucked in close to Nick on the bike, Rick heard the beautiful voice sing to him. He was ready to do his part.

Chapter 5

Reverend Scarecrow

Teresa DelVecchio parked her car on Lincoln Street next to her mother's bakery, grateful the rain had let up and the wind subsided. Though the dark clouds refused to relinquish their hold on the sky, dawn was sneaking a peek over the horizon. At least she and her two daughters would be able to dash into the bakery without getting soaked.

Mary Anne hurried back out to the front to greet the excited screams of her granddaughters. Before she made it through the doorway, Jessica and Bernadette had their grandmother surrounded with hugs. "Nana! Nana! We missed you!"

"Goodness me. This is the best welcome any Nana could get. How I've missed you. I'm glad you found your way back. You girls really know how to brighten up a gloomy day. Teresa, I'm delighted to see you as well."

Mary Anne and Teresa embraced each other warmly. Then Mary Anne turned to her granddaughters. "Help yourselves to breakfast and I'll be right with you. I want to hear all about your trip."

Jessica took Bernadette out front while Teresa followed her mother to the kitchen. "How was your week, Mom? Did I miss anything?"

"You missed a flurry earlier this morning. And, talk about excitement, you should have been here yesterday. Let's bring out these rolls and then grab a booth. We have some catching up to do."

Teresa hesitated. "We can chat right here, Mom, while I wash the baking trays. You have quite a stack in the sink."

"We can chat better in the café, honey. You have a fan club out there waiting to see you. I wasn't the only one who missed you, you know."

"Mother ..."

"Be brave, dear. Follow your mother."

Mary Anne grabbed Teresa's hand and pulled her out front, a tray of cinnamon rolls in her other hand. She caught a glimpse of her granddaughters playing with Rocco.

Rocco jumped to his feet as Teresa came through the door. "Welcome back, Teresa. It's good to see you again. I was hoping the weather wouldn't keep you away. I don't think your mother would have been able to handle it. She missed you terribly. And it was much too quiet around here without the girls."

He squirmed as he spoke, shifting from one foot to the other and his ears turned red. Teresa saw the redness creep silently up his neck and encompass his face, a sure sign that he knew he was rambling.

Teresa and Rocco had grown up in the village together. Their friendship had shifted through various stages from childhood buddies, to high school sweethearts, to their separate ways, and back to friendship. They had both agreed that they were too much like brother and sister to ever get married. Teresa had no trouble finding dates after that. Suitors stood in line for a chance to court her and her mother had a big job sizing them all up. She kept telling Teresa that she changed boyfriends like everyone else changed their socks. After each disappointing date, Teresa would call Rocco and complain to him about the creep she had gone out with. And Rocco always listened with unfeigned sympathy. Her mother kept telling her it was because Rocco was still in love with her … and vice versa. Teresa rolled her eyes every time.

"It's good to be back. Mom tells me that I missed some excitement around here yesterday."

"You sure did. But I'll let your Mom fill you in. Uncle Jake and I have to get over to the station and get a head start on the week's work."

Rocco looked down at the floor and continued, "Maybe you can hang around longer today. Deacon John just invited the girls to the Youth Rally. It's predicted to get sunny and warm this afternoon you know." By now his ears were a bright, cherry red, and beads of sweat were breaking out all over his forehead.

Mary Anne said, "I think I can twist her arm, Rocco. Maybe we can have our own 'Over the Hill Rally' at my place, while the girls enjoy themselves. Now get to work so you can finish up on time. Come on, Jake, you too. Fill a mug with coffee and move along."

Jake and Rocco filled their coffee mugs, and after leaving a generous tip, walked out of the bakery. Rocco paused at the door and glanced back at Teresa …

"He's sweet on you, Teresa, can't you tell? He's too shy to tell you, but it's written all over his ears."

"Oh, Mom. Rocco and I both agreed long ago that it wouldn't work. We did try. Don't you remember?"

"I remember you didn't try hard enough. He either gets tongue-tied or rambles like a fool whenever he's around you. Listen to your mother. He's available only for you, always has been. There'll never be anyone else who will match your stride."

"Rocco and I have a lot of fun together, Mom. We can't risk letting a romance destroy our friendship. That almost happened when we broke up the last time. But, I am looking forward to seeing him later at your place. So tell me, what happened this morning?"

"I'll tell you about that right after you fill me in about your trip. How was San Diego?"

"It was wonderful, Mom. The weather was perfect. Sunny and warm every day. And I met the nicest people at the conference. Dan Fletcher, a principal at a high school in San Diego, invited me to a diner during one of our breaks. He was interested in hearing about my experiences as a teacher in a country high school. We spoke for quite some time, comparing students and families from city schools and country schools and the problems each face. The parallels were amazing. We concluded that there are many more similarities than differences. Parents everywhere want their children to have the best and faith is an important factor."

"I agree with you and it begins the moment a child is born. The first time parents gaze at their newborn infant, they know they are gazing at eternity. It is like seeing life the way God does. There is no greater miracle."

"True. I remember feeling that way when Jessica and Bernadette were born. Dan said the same thing. Parents are pulling their children out of public schools and putting them into the New Life schools where faith and education merge. And these new schools cannot be built fast enough. He took me on a tour one evening after dinner and invited me to come back for an interview. I have to admit, it's tempting."

"Oh honey, you know I'd hate to see you have to go so far. I don't think I could stand it. Besides, there is plenty of moral decay right here in Hillcrest. The atmosphere in this town is changing, and I'm not talking about the weather. The gang that's been hanging around has been sending a chill through all the townspeople. The graffiti is making everything look shabby and dirty. And some of the residents, who have lived here all their lives, are beginning to talk about moving. Luke and Maddie are optimistic, though. You just missed them. They came earlier this morning, talking about establishing an interfaith school right here in town."

"So tell me, Mom. What has been happening around here?"

"Teresa, you should have been here yesterday…"

****

The storm clouds that had greeted the morning had long since vanished over the horizon. The gentle breeze that remained carried the laughter of the Holy Spirit Youth Committee across town, the hardiest laughter of all coming from Sister Madeleine. Not quite five feet tall and as jolly as she was round, Madeleine was the life of every party, even when she wasn't present, which was rare. Just the mention of her name brought peals of laughter and shared stories. She was known and loved by all the townspeople.

"I told you, I told you, I told you all. God always pulls through. Need I say more?" she sang, as she danced her way to one of the vans, carrying a picnic basket.

"You've said all that needs to be said, Maddie," laughed Father Luke. "God does indeed pull through for you."

"For you as well, dear brother of mine, and everyone else. You have only to listen in your heart to hear God's melody."

****

Father Luke and Sister Madeleine were both optimists by nature, but while Luke was aware of the dark clouds, Maddie focused on the silver lining. At gatherings, while Madeleine enjoyed being the center of attention, Luke preferred to watch from a silent corner. He wasn't aloof, just more comfortable on the sidelines with a smaller group, while Madeleine was comfortable everywhere; and wherever she was became the center. Luke was forever diving for cover while trying to keep her in his line of vision. They were inseparable despite frequent disagreements.

Both grew up with a strong faith and derived their strength from deep prayer and the sacraments. And both heard God calling them to religious life, but in different ways. Luke, who heard God call him to the priesthood, was a man of logic and reasoning. He believed everything could be explained and he wanted his flock to love their faith and know God as deeply as he did. But Luke was also searching. He knew about God but he didn't know God the way his sister did. He had never encountered God's presence in his life the way Madeleine had.

Madeleine, who had become a Sister of the Sacred Heart, heard God in her heart. Her favorite Bible story was about the Samaritan woman. The Holy Spirit, the fountain of living water, bubbled over within her into an enthusiastic and energetic outpouring of love for everyone. And it was contagious. The youth of the village were attracted to her and she wanted them to experience and love God the way she did. She knew there were people who would never come into church to find God so she took God on the road – into bars, onto baseball fields, into public schools. And she wasn't intimidated by the gang presence in the village. She even knew their names. Logan just glared at her the day she appeared in the center of their meeting wielding a large plastic bag filled with bottles of bubbles. He stood by helplessly as she passed them out to everyone. Though Logan refused to accept his, Gangster and Scar each obediently took a bottle. And while Logan stood by seething with anger, everyone blew bubbles and played and laughed for over an hour. Then Madeleine closed their recruitment meeting with a prayer and sent them home.

Father Luke almost had a stroke when she told him about it the next day.

"Are you mad? You're going to get yourself killed, Maddie. They'll come back for you and make it look like an accident."

"You worry too much, brother dear. We'll never get rid of them if we shiver from the sidelines. And they'll never come to church to be converted. We have to bring

God to them. If the youth know we're scared, it'll give the Jaguars more power."

"The Jaguars?"

"That's what they call themselves. They think it makes them sound tough. But don't forget, jaguars can only run fast for short bursts and then they run out of steam so we have time to catch up. Every time I infiltrate one of their meetings, I wear them down. Rabbi Silver agrees with me. He's coming with me on my next planned invasion."

"Maybe I'll come too."

"That would be great, Luke. It will take the whole United Pastoral Council together to chase them out of town. Just don't throw up on their boots, though, or you'll be the one they come after."

"Very funny, Maddie."

Luke and Maddie were the perfect complement to each other, like peanut butter and jelly. One cautious, the other carefree, one of mind, the other of heart, but both in love with God and his people.

****

"Melody, Maddie? Where did you come up with that one?"

"Face it, Luke. Faith and hope will end someday. Only love is eternal."

"You're right. And where did you learn that? The Good Book."

"Let her win this one, Padre. At least we can be up at Diamond Lake instead of in the church hall," said Jason Parente. "Let the good times roll."

76

His twin sister, Jackie, wasn't so sure, "What about the Jaguars? Sister Madeleine invited them. The good weather may encourage them to show up."

Jason put his arm around Jackie and said, "You're just upset because one of them keeps asking you out. He thinks you're hot." Jason laughed and began sashaying around, wiggling his hips.

Jackie scowled and pretended to gag, "Yuck! He's disgusting! He smells bad and he's got a scar on his face."

Sister Madeleine tried to give a reprimanding look, but on her cherubic face it looked like she was puckering for a kiss. "Now, now, Jackie. There's good in everyone. You just have to dig deep sometimes to find it. God didn't make anyone disgusting, not even your brother. I invited the gang to help us, but they are probably allergic to work. If they do have the nerve to show up we'll give them a job … down wind." Sister Madeleine chuckled. "And if we work them hard enough we'll either convert them or they'll never come back. It's a win-win scenario."

The twin's mother, Julie said, "I hope you're right, Maddie. At least there will be enough men there. Maybe that will discourage them."

Sister Madeleine answered, "Never fear, Julie dear. The one and only God who brought us the sunshine will also protect us. Don't forget that we have special friends in high places. We'll all have a great time, including the Jaguars."

Rabbi Silver chuckled and turned to the new pastor of Trinity Baptist. "And if the Jaguars dare to step out of line we have our own fire and brimstone preacher, the Very Reverend Gregory Marshall. Greg can always be counted on to pull a candle out of his hat, I mean, helmet. And I'll wager that he'll have the gang running before he even gets it lit."

Rabbi Silver slapped the young minister on his back. Reverend Marshall did indeed pull a candle out of his helmet and hold it up.

****

Only twenty-four years old, Gregory Marshall was the newly-ordained minister assigned to Trinity Baptist to replace their retiring pastor. The congregation had requested a young minister hoping to pry their youth away from their attraction to the gang. But they got more than they bargained for when they saw their new preacher ride into town on a motorcycle. And they were stunned speechless when he removed his helmet and leather jacket. He was a handsome man with penetrating blue eyes, shiny, long black hair pulled back into a tight ponytail, a perfectly trimmed beard and mustache, and a gold earring in each ear. They were even more dismayed when they saw his broad shoulders and muscular arms covered in tattoos. His one redeeming feature had been the large crucifix on a gold chain that he wore around his neck.

Reverend Gregory Marshall's first order of business, as the town youth excitedly gathered around his motorcycle, had been to pull a candle out of his helmet and light it. He then preached to those assembled about how Jesus was the light of the world and how the fire of His love should always burn brightly in their hearts. How the fire of that love saved and nourished them or judged with a deadly vengeance anyone who rejected Him.

His second order of business had been to infiltrate one of the after school gang meetings, light a candle in their midst, and preach the same message. Reverend Marshall was pleased with himself. He did break up the gang meeting but didn't realize that he was not discouraging anyone from wanting to join the Jaguars. He just changed the location of their meetings. They regrouped quickly in another location so they could entertain themselves by poking fun at the preacher who had a talent for scattering instead of gathering. Among his congregation and village youth, Gregory Marshall was dubbed Reverend Scarecrow.

The religious leaders knew that they had to act fast before he became a laughingstock to the whole village. The clergy and a group of parents met one morning at the bakery to discuss the best way to approach Greg without making him feel as if they were ganging up on him. Since he was new and younger than much of his congregation, they decided to host a casual dinner to get to know him better and speak about their concerns. Sister Madeleine, who happened to stop by the bakery for her morning coffee, joined the discussion. Looking around at the group, she informed them, "I think that the best approach to Greg should be a one-on-one. Anything else, no matter how informal, will appear to be ganging up."

Father Luke grinned at her. "You have that familiar sparkle in your eye, Maddie. You've already thought this one out, haven't you?"

"Thought out and strategized. Now all of you tell me what you think. Next Saturday morning, the Confirmation class is meeting in the church hall to design this year's Pascal Candle. I thought it might be the perfect time to invite Greg to help me and have him speak to the class. I could always use another pair of hands for these classes and Greg would fit right in. It would give him a chance to get to know us better. We'll end the class with a pizza lunch, and you're all invited.

Reverend John Burke, of St. Stephen Episcopal, was excited. "That's a great idea, Maddie. Maybe I can round up some of the youth from my parish. It would be good for Greg to see us working together. We'll bring dessert."

"Wonderful, John. Just let me know how many are coming so I can order enough pizza. Gerald, you come too, and bring your family. If Greg puts his candle in your face, I'll wrestle him to the ground and confiscate it."

Rabbi Silver laughed. "Thank you, Maddie. I'll look forward to it. My gang will bring beverages and maybe I'll even sport my own candle. Then Greg and I can have a gentlemen's duel."

After more discussion, the other ministers agreed to invite members from their youth groups. It was the best way for the new minister to experience the camaraderie that existed among all of the churches and the synagogue.

It turned out to be a plan made in heaven. And while the members of Trinity Baptist Church feared that they had gotten more than they bargained for, Sister Madeleine learned that their prayers had been answered in a bigger way than they could have imagined … or dared to believe. Gregory Marshall knew all about the Jaguars, because he had once been a member himself. He had had a secret reason for riding his motorcycle into the midst of one of their after school meetings. He wanted to see if any of members recognized him. Sister Madeleine roared with laughter as Greg described the gang's hasty retreat from him that day.

"You should have seen them take off, Maddie. They almost fell over their bikes trying to run away from me and my candle." Greg threw his head back and laughed. "Logan kept screaming 'Code Red, Beta'. He had a hard time maintaining control over the group and keeping his pants dry at the same time. It wasn't pretty."

Sister Madeleine doubled over laughing. "I think it was more the fire in your eyes than the flame on the candle that had them running." She took a tissue out of her pocket, wiped her eyes, and blew her nose. "By the way, what does 'Code Red, Beta' mean?"

"It means head for the hills."

"I won't waste my time asking if they recognized you. They probably never gave time for lightning to strike."

"I'd be very surprised if they recognize me now, even if they came to my church and sat through a whole service. They haven't seen me since they left me for dead six years ago. Would you believe me if I told you that in high school, I was a scrawny, clumsy geek who got straight A's in every subject … except phys-ed? I had a squeaky voice, greasy black hair, zits all over my face, a mouth full of metal, and thick, very thick, glasses. I couldn't find my way out of a bathroom stall without them."

Sister Madeleine stopped moving chairs and made the time out sign with her hands. "Back up there, partner, and explain the part about being left for dead." She grasped Greg's arm and led him to a row of chairs where they both sat down. "How did you go from pimply blind scrawny geek to not breathing to handsome prince with a motorcycle and candle ministry?"

Sister Madeleine watched the redness creep up his neck and said to him, "Don't worry, Greg. You're among friends here … family, in fact. Whatever you say here stays here, unless you choose to speak of it. I'd like to get to know you better since you're now part of our interfaith team."

Greg closed his eyes for a minute to compose himself. He folded his hands in his lap, and when he opened his eyes, Maddie saw that they were red, but he took a deep breath and shared his story.

"It is a time in my life that I'd rather put behind me. I was an embarrassment to myself and my parents, especially my father, who was also a preacher. I just wish he could see me now, Maddie."

"I'm sure he does, Greg, and I'm just as sure he is proud of you."

"I hope so. Every father wants his son to follow his example and I never gave him a clue that I would. I rebelled against everything he preached and even stopped going to church. He was upset with me and it caused some terrible arguments between my parents. My mother never lost hope, though. She just kept telling him that I was going through a phase and that I'd eventually come to my senses. Isn't there a saint in your church for my case?"

"Yes there is, Greg. In the fourth century, Monica prayed and chased her son Augustine all over the known world for years. She refused to give up. And when he did convert, he gave himself totally to God. Mother and son are both canonized. There is another example, also, right in Sacred Scripture. Do you remember the parable of the prodigal son? In that story it is the father who never loses hope and plans a welcome home party even before his son has a chance to ask for forgiveness. The next time you sit down to pray, thank your father for his patience and guidance. He doesn't need it, but you do. It will deepen your healing. Tell me more. You still haven't gotten to the part about being left for dead."

"That was the hardest part for both of my parents. I didn't really fit in anywhere in high school. I was awkward and shy. Then this gang started showing up after school and hanging around. They really seemed to like me and I really liked their motorcycles. It wasn't long before I learned to ride and wanted one of my own. For the first time in my life I felt like I belonged, that I was in the right place. And it was so exciting! I was having the time of my life until they gave me a 'special job' to prove my allegiance to them and earn a promotion. They even promised to give me my own motorcycle. I was hooked. All I had to do was rob a liquor store. And it was going to be easy because the owner's son was a secret member of the gang and he planned to leave the back door unlocked. All I had to do was sneak in and carry out a case of booze. No one was going to get hurt. But Mom was right. The roots of their upbringing were planted deeply and I couldn't bring myself to do it. And I was afraid of what they would demand next, so I pulled out."

"It must have taken a lot of courage to walk away from them."

"It sure did. All of my insides had turned to mush when I had to explain my failure to the leader the next day after school. A couple of new recruits who were eager to prove their loyalty dragged me into the woods behind the school, beat me, and left me for dead. I woke up in a hospital bed three days later. Fortunately, it happened right at the end of the school year so I didn't have to go back. I was allowed to recuperate and finish my schoolwork at home. Mom and dad were great. Neither of them ever said 'I told you so.'"

Sister Madeleine chuckled. "My brother, Luke, is not so fortunate. I say that to him all the time. He says it's my mantra. He'll be here soon, by the way. He comes over every Saturday to help with my faith formation class, so you'll get to know him a little better, too. Let's finish setting up while you finish your story. How did you go from being left at death's doorstep to Prince Charming?"

Greg relaxed and continued, "While I recovered, my parents wouldn't let me do much except lie around, so I had a lot of time to think … and reflect. One of the last things I remembered was seeing a large rock closing in on me and my last thought was a screaming plea to Jesus. In my dreams, I walked with the Lord along a stretch of shoreline and, just before he vanished, he would hand me a lighted candle and tell me to spread the Good News. I know he saved me and I promised the rest of my life to him. After

84

high school, I went right into Divinity Seminary. And now, here I am, Reverend Scarecrow, minister of fire and brimstone, at your service."

The students arriving at the church hall for their religion class saw Sister Madeleine and Reverend Marshall doubled over with laughter. The class that followed was the best ever.

Chapter 6

Transcending Death

Sam stood and gathered Joseph, Matthew, and James around him and called his mother to join them. He looked at each boy, his peaceful, radiant expression instilling in them a sense of security. "Do you remember when Jesus said to his apostles that where two or three were gathered in his name, he was there among them? He wanted them to know that they were never alone in their trials. The same is true for you boys. Keep listening to God in your hearts and trust him. Difficult circumstances are no obstacle to God's grace. You must follow the Father's lead and dig deep to discover the treasure of answered prayer. Most of the time victory arrives when least expected so don't blink or you'll miss the fireworks. Now let us confide ourselves and our plans to Abba."

As they bowed their heads in prayer, Matthew was the first to notice the magnificent rainbow that embraced the entire sky.

"Look!" he exclaimed, running to the window, "Isn't a rainbow a sign of God's promise? Maybe God is trying to tell us something."

"Yes, he is, genius," Joseph answered. He couldn't help himself. "He's trying to tell you that it stopped raining. It's time to jet."

Sam turned to Martha and hugged her. "Keep the home fires burning, Mama. Me and the team here are comin' back."

"I've heard that before. Just make sure you take care of my new friends. Don't let them out of your sight."

"Aye, aye, Captain Mommy." Sam saluted his mother and led the three boys to the front door.

Martha hugged each one and encouraged them. "Be careful. Do whatever Sam tells you and stay close to him. Most of all come back. I'll be here waiting and anxious."

Sam reached for the doorknob and looked back at Martha. He said with a twinkle in his eye, "A pot of your delicious soup on the home fires would be most welcome. We'll be able to use our noses to find our way home. I remember reading somewhere once that leaving a trail of breadcrumbs doesn't work."

Martha chuckled. She opened the door and gave him a shove. "Just keep your mind on your task right now and let me tend the home fires."

****

As Sam led the boys to the footbridge toward the base of Mount Gilead, Sheriff Al Benson and Officer Ed Pagano pulled into the main entrance of the Diamond Lake Cabin Colony.

"This is going to be like looking for a grasshopper in a cornfield, Al. We'll never find those boys today, especially with the rally going on. There must be over three hundred people here already."

"And more are coming, Ed. This annual youth rally has become the biggest event of the year. One thing we have going for us is that the three boys will probably stick together, and two of them have red hair. You don't see too many redheads. We'll just keep our eyes open. The whole force is on duty today."

"Did you see the photograph? They don't look like your typical runaways. I bet they couldn't survive long on their own."

"That's what we're counting on. They should be easy to spot in a crowd."

"Why did they run away?"

"Well, the notice we received from VFPD informed us that they ran away from a foster home because they didn't want to be split up. Gordon Munson from CPS told me they couldn't find a home that would take them together. Two of the boys are teenagers and the little one is only six. That puts many people off. And their foster mother said they're a real handful."

"They look like nice boys from their photo. Mary Anne said they were real polite to her. Her heart went out to them."

Al laughed. "You know she's such a soft touch, Ed. Once we catch them, though, we'll see for ourselves. Like I said, they shouldn't be too hard to spot. First thing we have to do is touch base with the deacon. If those boys are hiding out here somewhere, they may try to blend in with the rally to grab some food and dart back out. That's what I'd do if I were in their shoes."

Ed laughed. "I'd like to see you run in their shoes. What a sight that would be. You'd be the easy catch."

"I doubt it. You and everyone else would probably be laughing too hard to come after me, funny boy. I'd get away."

James slowed his steps as they came closer to the footbridge and looked back toward the cabin, an anxious expression clouding his face. Joseph noticed and went back to him. "What's up, little brother?"

"Nothing."

Joseph noticed his brother's lower lip tremble and put his arm around him. "It's okay. Come on. Hop on my back and I'll carry you across."

James took a step back. "Maybe I'll just wait here for you."

Matthew, who had been leaning over the railing, watching the rushing water flow over the rocks, called to his brothers. "This is so cool. You have to see this up close. I never heard water make this much noise. It sounds like thunder."

James took another step back and looked up at Joseph. "I think someone should stay with Martha, so she's not lonely, you know."

Sam, a huge smile on his face, raised his arms and began dancing on the bridge. He sang,

"It's time to dance across the bridge.
It's time to climb the highest ridge.
There is no danger of a fall.
God can hold us one and all."

All three boys laughed as Sam danced his way to James, turned his back to him, squatted, and said, "Hop aboard, James the Great. You and I will skip across, while your brothers watch, green with envy."

James hopped on and wrapped himself tightly around Sam, who danced across the footbridge, still singing his song.

****

Martha watched from the window and grinned. Sam had a way with children. His standing bet with her was that he could get the most fearful child laughing within a minute. It was a bet he never lost.

Grief was a different story, however, especially in children who had lost their parents under tragic circumstances. Their pain, sadness, and sense of loss cut deeper than any other emotion and their ability to trust was shattered. They knew intuitively that no one else could love and accept them as their parents. Even when placed with a loving family, it took a long time to heal. Waking up every morning and remembering ... but at least these boys had each other. Martha prayed for their prayer to be answered.

****

Joseph and Matthew skipped next to Sam, all of them singing their new song, their voices rising above the deafening roar of the rushing water below. They reached the other side and continued on to the base of Mount Gilead. The wet grass and mud squished under their feet, kicking up muddy water against the backs of their jeans. Only James stayed dry perched up on Sam's back, his chin resting on Sam's shoulder.

****

Peering through the brush at the jogger's entrance to the cabin colony, two police officers observed three boys running across a footbridge and vanishing into the shrubs at the base of the mountain. One of the officers pulled out his radio and reported to Sheriff Benson.

"Al, we've spotted the boys. They are approaching the base of Mount Gilead, right across from the deserted cabin at the end of the woods. Should we go in after them?"

"Just tail them for now and report back. I'll send in more men and then we'll apprehend them. Maintain radio silence until you find out where they're hiding. Good work."

"Thanks, Chief. We're on our way."

****

Sheriff Benson clicked off his radio and put it back on his belt. "Well, they were easy to find. Hopefully they'll be as easy to catch."

"There are a couple of caves along the way up Gilead. Those boys may have taken shelter from last night's storm in one, probably the first one."

"I think they're just exploring, Ed. They probably spent the night in that deserted cabin. I'll station a couple of men in the woods near each entrance to the cabin in case the boys go back there."

****

When they reached the base of the mountain, Sam put James down and gathered the boys around him.

"Now begins the hard part. The ground is soaked and the rocky surfaces will be slick. We can take our time climbing. The trees should provide us with enough cover even if the police come in the same way you boys did. So take it easy and keep your voices low. Our song ends here for now."

Joseph asked, "Won't they see us when we get to the top?"

Sam said, "We won't be going all the way up. In fact, we'll be stopping just short of the top. I am taking you to a place that was very special to me when I was your age, my own heaven on earth. It's easy to get lost in its beauty. I used to spend hours there talking to God and thinking. Abba used to lift my spirit higher than an eagle's flight. If you like it as much as I did, you won't want to come back down. And there is a cave nearby we can explore."

Sam saw the fear creep into James' face. He leaned over and whispered into his ear, "Don't worry, James the Great, we'll send Matthew in first to scare the bears and bats out."

Matthew laughed as they started their climb. He said, "It would be my pleasure. The bears and bats won't stand a chance."

Again, Joseph couldn't help himself. "Especially when you dazzle them with your four-letter preaching."

James hesitated. "Sam, why do you call me James the Great? I'm not so great."

93

Sam answered, "I call you James the Great because you display such courage. You and your brothers made it this far because you did your part despite the risks. Keep up the good work, my friend."

By this time, they had reached the first clearing which was covered with a layer of smooth, flat rocks. "This is one of two places on the way up that is a bear to cross. Bend your knees and put your weight on the balls of your feet so you don't slip or twist an ankle. Take your time."

The rocks glistened from the rain and there were puddles in the crevices. Sam showed the boys how to squat low and creep along without slipping. At one point, however, Matthew's foot slipped out from under him and he fell forward and hit his head. He got right up and tried to act as if it was nothing, but Sam could see the dazed look and tears he was struggling to hold back. In a move swifter than a flash of lightning, Sam grabbed Matthew and swung him onto his back. "Bet you didn't know I had it in me, huh? You're never too big for a piggyback ride." Sam's booming laughter echoed back from earth and sky.

He put his arm around Matthew's head and held him close. The stunned look on Matthew's face was so comical that his brothers couldn't help but laugh. "Sam, I've never seen Matthew look so confused and I bet it's more from suddenly finding himself on your back than hitting his head on that rock," said Joseph.

A small bruise on Matthew's forehead had started to bleed. Joseph pulled a tissue out of his pocket and wiped the blood. When he pulled his hand away, there was no sign of the bruise. A small spot of blood on the tissue was the only evidence that there had been a wound. Joseph kept looking from Matthew's forehead to the tissue. Now he was the one stunned.

James asked, "What happened, Joe?"

Joseph kept staring at the tissue. "I'm not sure. Maybe it was just dirt. But there's no dirt on the tissue, only blood; and such a tiny speck."

Sam beamed at them, his eyes glistening. "We all have the power to heal within us. And that tissue is now a sign. Treasure it, my friend. No hurt is too big or too small for the power of love."

Joseph folded the tissue, carefully tucking the spot of blood to the inside, and put it into his pocket. No one spoke ... or moved. Instead, they found themselves lost in the bliss of the moment, as if frozen in time. Then angels gathered round, dancing and singing praise to the glory of the Lamb, their joyous melody whispering in the uppermost branches and leaves of the surrounding trees. Their whirling dance creating a breeze that caressed the faces of Sam and the boys, nourishing their souls.

The police officer, hiding behind an outcropping of rock, also felt the breeze but only saw three boys sitting on a large rock surveying their surroundings. And while Joseph, Matthew, and James were rapt in the presence of the sacred, Sam recalled the moment that had made this ground forever sacred ... remembering because he had been there himself. It was hard to believe that almost two hundred years had gone by. Even though the mission had been a success, the path of events leading up to its fulfillment appeared destined for disaster. The disciples were brand new in the faith but had faced their challenge with courage and conviction.

****

In 1824, Chief Lone Hawk had been leading his people up this mountain to a cave just below the summit carrying an important manuscript. Sam and six youths of the tribe were bringing up the rear and protecting the women who were just ahead of them. In the place where Joseph, Matthew, and James now stood, one of the villagers, who had been following, hurled a knife, plunging it into the neck of the chief's daughter.

As she fell to the ground and the women gathered around her, five of the youths turned back to chase the man who could be heard retreating in a raging panic, stumbling through the brush and tripping over roots and rocks, his heart pounding through his chest like the approaching thunder of a herd of wild horses. He didn't care if he got caught. He wanted to die now, anyway. The gentle dove who now lay dying on the cold stone surface of the mountain was the love of his life. Maybe was already dead because of his stubborn impulsiveness. *What an idiot! How could he have missed the tree?* All he wanted to do was scare them. Let them know that he was just as tough as they were. That he was good enough to be counted among them. *Why was he even running?* His last thought as he fell was the realization that he wasn't so tough. Tough men don't cry. But even that didn't matter anymore.

They had dragged him back, one on each side, barely lifting him high enough to keep his face from scraping the ground and tied him up against the tree that had been his intended victim. Then Sam stood in their midst, in silence, present as the calm eye at the heart of their rage, standing with them as they tried to reconcile their righteous anger with their newborn faith; standing with them in union with Father and Spirit. They had no weapons. The villager was safe for the moment. And Rosebud was safe as well. Her blood barely had time to warm the rock beneath her when a cry rose up from those gathered round. She was sitting up now, the women cheering, her mother crying, wailing, tears streaming down her face, her eyes closed, her arms clutching Rosebud tightly to her bosom. Her younger brother, who had dropped to her side as she fell, was staring in stunned disbelief from Rosebud's neck to the blanket he had grabbed to staunch the flow of blood. When he pulled the blanket away, there was no sign of the wound ... or the knife. A small spot of blood on the blanket was the only evidence that there had been an injury.

Everyone gathered around Rosebud then. When her older brothers saw her sitting up, they ran over to her. Her father lifted her in his arms, hugging her tightly, his arms also around his wife. Both of them crying now, joyfully ... thanking God, praising him. Sam beamed at them, standing in the circle, his eyes glistening. "We all have the power to heal within us. And that blanket is now a sign. Treasure it, my friends. No hurt is too big or too small for the power of love."

To the tribute of the whole group, and especially of Rosebud's brothers, they forgave the young villager and expressed their gratitude to God for restoring their sister to them. Sam had been so proud of them that day. Had the young men given in to their rage, justified as it was, the mission would have failed. And the world would never have known. Sam could read the struggle in their faces, could see it in their hearts. But they chose to remain steadfast and were victorious. Love and mercy triumphed, as did justice and honor. The young man did not return to the village, instead remaining with the tribe and accepting their way of life. The power of love to heal had touched them all. To mark the event, Chief Lone Hawk had named the mountain Gilead.

****

Sam was the first to rouse himself from his reverie. It was time to move on.

"Rest time is over, boys. Let's keep going. I can't wait for you to see my special place. We'll take a longer rest up there."

Matthew tried to get down but Sam held him fast.

"A ride is a ride, Reverend Valente, and you haven't gotten my money's worth yet. Stay tucked in now and enjoy the view."

As they continued their climb, James giggled every time he looked up at Matthew. But Joseph was silent, lost in thought. Finally, he asked, "What happened, Sam? There was a bruise on Matthew's forehead. We all saw it."

Sam draped an arm around Joseph's shoulder. "When we get to the top, I'll have a story to tell you that will help you understand. It was something I was just musing over myself."

****

Sam and the boys continued to climb. Six more police officers arrived at the base of the mountain. Two more crossed over the footbridge and stationed themselves outside each entrance to Cabin 33. Officer Bill Bennett assigned two of the policemen to remain behind while he took the rest to meet up with the first officer. They had not gone far when they met Officer Leo Colombe on his way back down.

"They vanished into thin air," he informed the group. "I rounded a bend in the trail and they were gone. I don't even know how that was possible. They were in my sight the whole time, and even when they got farther ahead, I could still hear them."

"Maybe they knew they were being followed and ducked into a cave," suggested Bill.

"I don't think so," said Leo. "They were not even near a cave when they disappeared. It's the strangest thing."

"Strange for you, Leo," said Bill. "You've never lost anyone you were tailing, but there is a first time for everything, even for you. Don't be so hard on yourself. They'll turn up. They have to be up here somewhere."

"Maybe not," said Ralph. "I'll bet they did know they were being tailed and doubled back. Did you, by any chance, look behind you?"

"What do you think I'm doing now, RALPH?!" said Leo, the anger rising in his voice.

"Relax, Leo. It's no big deal. We'll find them," said Bill.

"And we'll give you the credit. Don't worry, Leo, your secret's NOT safe with us," said Ralph, continuing to taunt him.

"That's enough, Ralph," said Bill. "We have a job to do here and we need to work together."

There had been tension between Leo and Ralph since their graduation from the Police Academy a year ago. They had been the best of friends through high school and had entered the Academy together. Just before graduation, Ralph discovered that his girlfriend was also dating Leo. He was crushed to learn that Jennifer had been using him to get to Leo. But the relationship hadn't worked out for her either. Leo was competitive by nature and vain about his appearance. Once he got what he wanted, the challenge was over, and he moved on to his next conquest.

Ralph knew that losing the three boys he was tailing would continue to gnaw at Leo and he was going to ride it as far as he could. Payback was going to be sweet. He had to be careful, however, because he had a tendency to go too far. More often than not, he stretched his boundaries too far and found himself in deep weeds. And the risks were much higher now. He had worked hard to get a place on the force. He hoped he wouldn't get too carried away. God help him … He would have to, because once he got going, he wouldn't be able to help himself.

****

Sam and the boys climbed the rest of the way without incident. The sun was peeking out through the parting clouds, giving everything a fresh, clean appearance.

And the angels were doing their part, veiling Sam and the boys from sight after they rounded the bend in the trail. Sam chuckled to himself when he glanced over his shoulder and saw Leo staring into thin air, his hat in his hand, squinting as if daring them to reappear, then angrily slamming his hat to the ground and pounding the air.

****

Sister Madeleine watched Deacon John approach her serving table, looking angrier than a hornet caught between a window and a screen on a hot, summer day.

"What's up, John? I'd suggest that you put a bag of ice under your cap but I'm afraid it would turn to steam before it had a chance to cool you off."

John sputtered, "I think Al's lost touch with reality. He wants us to forget about the gang and focus on those runaways. But they're not the ones who are going to cause trouble around here today."

"Why would he tell you to do that?"

"Because they've been spotted heading toward Gilead. Bill and Leo were hiding in the brush and saw them crossing the footbridge, heading toward the mountain. They may have spent the night in a nearby cabin. Al thinks they're just exploring right now but they may try to blend in with the youth here to get food."

"Well, I hope they do show up. They need to eat and they're probably starved. Don't worry, John, that gang won't cause any trouble. We have a record number of parents here. Just focus on your message to the youth and the special project you have planned for them this summer. I'm sure it'll go over big time and keep them distracted from the gang all summer. Who knows? Maybe the Jaguars won't get any new recruits and will get bored enough to leave town. Even better, maybe God and I will join and really give them a run for their money."

Deacon John chuckled. "You always know how to put things in the proper perspective, Maddie. I should have come to you before I let anything get to me. Has everyone eaten yet?"

"Everyone except the workers. Some of the youth are still coming back for seconds, thirds, and beyond. It's good to see them enjoying themselves and talking about their summer plans. The teachers and principals of both the middle and high schools have been telling the youth how proud they are of them. A record number of students made the honor roll this year. As a reward, there are a couple of field trips planned for the last week of school. And the Ice Cream Shoppe is giving the honor students free ice cream cones on field day."

"What a great idea! By the way, have you spied any gang members around?"

"Not so far, John, unless they are out of uniform. I don't think I'd recognize them if they were wearing baseball caps like the rest of the youth. Why don't you grab yourself a plate and join Luke. He's sitting in the pavilion with Mary Anne's granddaughters. I'll join you in a minute myself. My shift is almost over."

"Good idea, Maddie. The food looks great! Who's cooking?"

"The committee from Temple Abraham. And they've been having a great time with Greg. He had the nerve to ask them if they had any kosher hotdogs and they handed him one on a stick with lit a candle for him to cook it over."

They both laughed as Deacon John filled his plate. Sister Madeleine heaped more food on when she thought he hadn't taken enough.

"If you fatten me up too much, Mom, I won't be able to chase after the gang," he teased her.

"You just enjoy the picnic right now, son, and let God take care of the gang. His angels can fly faster than their motorcycles can jet," she shot back.

Sister Madeleine laughed to herself as John walked toward the pavilion. She loved it when they called her Mom.

****

Matthew turned to Sam and said, "I see the second cave, Sam, at the end of this path."

Sam nodded. "We are very close now, boys, to my special place. And it just appears that the trail has ended but it continues between those two trees. Everyone who hikes up this trail stops here to rest and then heads back down. But we'll continue on and I'll tell you about a group of people who made this mountain forever sacred …"

103

CHAPTER 7

Transfigured

Jake stood at the counter in Mary Anne's kitchen whipping potatoes while Mary Anne heated milk and melted butter into a pan on the stove.

"If I didn't know better, I'd think you were trying to cozy up Teresa and Rocco."

"What makes you think that, Jake?" said Mary Anne distractedly, gazing out her kitchen window, a pensive smile curling up the corners of her mouth.

"Because I'm standing here doing Teresa's job while she is outside weeding your flower garden ... with Rocco. I wasn't born yesterday, Mare. You're about as subtle as a chainsaw."

"It couldn't have been that obvious. It didn't take much to get them out there and you didn't put up much of an argument when I handed you the beaters. Teresa and Rocco just need a gentle push in the right direction."

"It was more like a shove. You know, I wasn't too surprised when Teresa didn't come home after college. Then she went off and married that feller from the Navy. They were so happy together. Too bad he died."

"True. Teresa enjoyed all the moving and traveling that went with Ben's position. And she never had trouble finding a job but I think she's ready to settle down now and I hope it's here. I'd hate to think that she'd consider Dan Fletcher's invitation. I'd miss her too much."

"I don't think she's serious about his offer. She doesn't want her daughters so far away from you either and she'd miss you just as much."

"I hope you're right."

"I don't think you have anything to worry about, Mare. She may have had an exciting trip, but she was more excited to get back and tell you about it. She's a little older now, a little more grown up; not the same happy-go-lucky teenager who wanted to see the world. And, don't forget, tragedy has a way of carving you deeper. I have noticed a more serene quality about her that wasn't there before."

Mary Anne stopped stirring and stared out the window again. "I've noticed it myself. Maybe I don't have to fret." She smiled and added, "But a friendly nudge in the right direction can't hurt."

Jake returned the smile. "You mean shove."

Jake joined Mary Anne at the window and they watched Teresa and Rocco sitting back on their feet laughing. Rocco, red-faced as usual, had a clothespin on his nose.

Jake said, "I wonder what's so funny."

"I know what they're laughing at. They smell a skunk and must have figured out that the scent is coming from the flowers. The Women's Guild was giving away skunk flower bulbs free at Town Hall one day and I picked up a few."

Jake looked quizzically at her. "Why would you want to grow flowers that stink?"

"Because squirrels can't stand the smell of a skunk. If you plant them in the tulip patch, it will keep the squirrels from digging up the tulips bulbs and eating them. Don't tell me you never heard of skunk bulbs before."

"New one on me, Mare. I always wondered why I smelled skunks more in the daytime in spring than in summer. I just thought they stayed awake more during the day from hibernating all winter. You have a beautiful flowerbed, even if it does stink. I suppose if roses have thorns to protect them, tulips can have stinky flowers to protect them."

"True. And it's certainly providing some good entertainment right now."

Mary Anne removed the pan of milk and butter from the stove and poured it in a thin stream into the potatoes, while Jake continued to whip them.

"The secret to delicious mashed potatoes," she informed Jake, "is to melt the butter into the milk, and then pour the mixture in a thin stream into the potatoes while they are hot, to reduce lumps and whip them up nice and fluffy."

"The secret to delicious mashed potatoes," Jake informed Mary Anne, "is to get invited to your place, Mare. They're perfect every time."

"I didn't realize mashing potatoes could be so entertaining," said Teresa, as she walked through the back door with Rocco.

"Almost as entertaining as a stinky flower garden," observed Mary Anne. "It was nice to see you and Rocco having such a good time. And, Rocco, that clothespin on your nose suited you. Maybe you should make it part of your wardrobe."

Jake chimed in, "That's a great idea. Don't they even come in colors? You could wear a different color every day."

Mary Anne watched the redness slowly creep over his face and softened his discomfit by asking them both to set the table. "As soon as Jake recovers from his surprising moment of wisdom and hilarity and finishes his assignment," she narrowed her eyes and gave Jake a hard stare, "everything will be ready for our special dinner. Rocco and Teresa, will you two set the table? Don't forget the candles and the wine glasses for we are celebrating."

"What are we celebrating, Mom? I didn't know this was a special occasion."

"Of course it is, dear. Today we are celebrating us, our friendship. Here we are on this beautiful day! What could be better than that? It's been a while since the four of us have gotten together and I just can't get over the feeling that it means more this time. And, Jake, if you make a wisecrack about woman's intuition, you won't get any of those delicious mashed potatoes you've worked so hard on."

"You are right, Mom. Up till now, I've been tempted by Dan's offer to teach out west but it doesn't feel right anymore. Do you know what I mean? I would miss all of you too much if I moved that far away. And Rocco, you've been my best friend as far back as I can remember. Thank you for being here today."

"I do understand, Teresa." Mary Anne put the empty pan in the sink and wiped her hands on her apron. "I hope you find a job nearby. I'd miss you too much as well."

Teresa put her arms around Rocco and kissed his cheek. Mary Anne watched his redness deepen and sensed a deepening of their friendship … and need for each other. *Please God!*

Jake added, "As far as I'm concerned, and I am, anytime we get together is a reason to celebrate. Thank you for your generous hospitality and good food, Mare. And those are my final words of wisdom for the day. Hopefully the hilarity will continue."

Teresa and Rocco gathered the tablecloth, candles, and wine glasses and went out to the deck to set the table, while Jake scooped the mashed potatoes into a heated bowl. Mary Anne hummed a tune as she reached for the bottle of wine she had picked up in town … and she prayed …

The hilarity did indeed continue.

****

Father Luke and Deacon John watched Jessica and Bernadette skip toward the community room.

"Wouldn't it be great if Teresa moved back to Hillcrest, Luke? I think the girls would settle in pretty fast and Teresa is such an inspiring teacher. She really knows how to motivate her students."

"That would be great but I don't know if she'll ever settle down. Do you remember how animated she was whenever they came back from anywhere? She would be energized and full of ideas. And she loved going wherever her husband's career took her. So did Bernadette and Jessica. It's the only kind of life they've known. Hillcrest would probably put them into a coma."

"There comes a time when that kind of life gets pretty old. She sure would be great on the planning committee for our new school. There could be enough excitement for her and the girls right here. Who knows?

Maybe we'll even get Rocco on the committee," said John, breaking into a huge grin.

"The shock of that would lay me low. Now let's get over to the community room ourselves. You need time to get into character for your talk."

Both men walked toward the community room where the youth were gathering to hear about their surprise summer adventure. Sister Madeleine stood at the door as they entered and refused give them a clue what the surprise was about. Only the twinkle in her eye told them they would be hanging on every word Deacon John spoke. Reverend Gregory Marshall stood on the other side of the door handing out programs.

Unseen by everyone, the room was also filling with the angelic host of the heavens. Their precious melody increased the sense of joyful anticipation among the youth; their presence intensified the aura of celebration for the whole town was part of the special mission. The town was beloved of God because their love for each other had transcended the boundaries of race, creed, and status.

The timing for the meeting was perfect as well. After a day full of food and games even the youth were ready to settle down for the moment.

****

Deacon John Salerno came and stood before them then, dressed in the garments of his Native American heritage. The youth gazed at him in wonder and awe. They knew of his ancestral background because of the stories he had told them but had never seen him dressed in his native

110

attire. His shiny black hair, which was normally pulled back in a ponytail or long thick braid, was now parted into two long braids, one on each side of his head. A streak of white paint over each cheek gave his face a sculpted look and made his dark eyes even more penetrating. The band that wound around his head contained a single feather in hues of blue and purple, shimmering in the fading rays of the setting sun. His brown fringed jacket and trousers blended into the wood surroundings so well that, except for his white face paint and glistening eyes, he was almost invisible. No one heard or saw him enter the room. His moccasins glided across the wood floor as silently as leaves falling from a tree. Only his smile gave him away. He stood there filled with anticipation and excitement, the joy and exhilaration of achieving a long sought after dream.

He had spent nearly three years researching his ancestral background. He wanted there to be no doubt concerning the information he was about to share. And Father Luke had provided unwavering support. He accepted him when he requested Holy Spirit Parish for his pastoral assignment, allowed him to continue his research, helped him with his studies, offered resources and encouragement, granted him permission to travel to the Vatican … and shared his enthusiasm when he returned.

Now the time for revelation had finally arrived. Deacon John Salerno stood before everyone and held up the peace stick he had been holding down by his side. Silence enveloped the room as gently as ripples spreading across a pond reaching every corner and heart.

Even the angels surrounding the room gathered in respectful pose, their music silenced for the moment.

111

Laying the peace stick at his feet, John put his hands together in prayer and reverently bowed his head, praying for courage and guidance. Then, picking up the stick, he began, his heart pounding in his chest.

"Thank you all for coming here today. I hope you all had a great time."

He laid the peace stick on the floor and applause and cheering filled the room.

Silence returned as he picked it back up, a visible sign of their uncompromising respect for each other.

"You all know of my Native American heritage and have always been attentive to the stories I've shared with you about my people. There is a part of my background, however, that I had not been able to share with you until now because the information I uncovered was too uncertain. But it was also the reason I came here to Hillcrest. Father Luke graciously accepted my request to be assigned here and all of you have been most hospitable. I am humbled and grateful. Now my research is complete and I am anxious to share it with you. It is our surprise summer project in which, I hope, you all will join me.

"This cabin colony is built on sacred ground. Almost two hundred years ago, a group of my people became converts to the Christian faith. They had hoped to remain with their tribe but their people could not accept their new way of worshipping God. They faced intense persecution. Their lives were in constant danger and so they had to flee.

"One night they escaped and arrived here on this land. They took nothing with them, not even weapons, in accord with Sacred Scripture. Nearby there was a village where Hillcrest now stands. The people who lived there befriended my ancestors and helped them get settled in their new life. I have also learned that I am a direct descendant of the leader of the tribe, Chief Lone Hawk.

"They lived in peace for a number of years. But, it is here that their story abruptly ends. The only other thing that I can tell you is that somewhere up in Mount Gilead they hid a manuscript which describes their way of life and the blessings they received from the hands of God. Soon afterward they disappeared. We don't know if they decided to move, were chased off this land, or were attacked and killed. The fact that they hid a manuscript does tell us that there was some kind of trouble and they wanted to preserve evidence of their existence.

"It is my hope that all of you will help me search for this manuscript. I also have to admit that its existence is not certain but a letter I came across during my recent trip to the Vatican Archives mentions such a manuscript and Chief Lone Hawk by name. It was written by a young man from the village to his family informing them of his decision to remain with the tribe and embrace their culture and faith. And, for now, that is where my story ends. Thank you for your generous attention. I will lay the peace stick down and answer any of your questions."

For a few seconds no one stirred, a moment frozen in time, like a snapshot. Then John noticed that Sister Madeleine and Greg were moving to the back of the room. They stopped near where Nick was sitting with his brother Rick on his lap. Rick had his hands folded and his eyes closed; a look of rapture animated his face. John knew that Nick was one of the youth who wanted to join the

Jaguars and was involved in the attack on the three boys the day before. Was it only yesterday? It seemed eons ago. They had been so busy planning for the rally and now the day was almost over. Nick had been helpful throughout the day and attentive to his brother. And the angelic look on Rick's face made him wonder if he was tuned in to another world …

Jason Parent drew Deacon John's attention back to the room. "How soon can we get started?"

The room, again, erupted in thunderous applause. Everyone rose to their feet cheering. Deacon John put his hands together and bowed to the audience.

"Thank you all. Your generous response is awe-inspiring. We will have to be patient until the school year is complete before we begin our search of the grounds and mountain but we will meet together in the church hall in the next couple of weeks to plan our strategy. Each of your churches and the synagogue will let you know when the meetings are scheduled. Thank you from the depth of my spirit." And Deacon John again bowed to his audience.

****

Sam led Joseph, Matthew, and James past the second cave and between two trees where the path continued to rise and curve. Just as the path seemed to end, Sam bent over and lifted up a thick overhanging vine as if opening a secret trap door. The boys stepped through with Sam following close behind.

The scene the boys stepped into was breathtaking. They found themselves in a small clearing surrounded by tall trees, flowering shrubs, and a thick carpet of velvety green grass invitingly ripe for bare feet. Birds chirped in the trees. Rabbits hopped about on the lush lawn nibbling on colorful flowers. Squirrels and chipmunks scurried across the grass chasing each other up and down trees and around the bushes. Large, puffy white clouds floated across the vast expanse of the cerulean sky. The scene was incredibly beautiful and tranquil ... and familiar.

Matthew was the first to speak up, "This looks just like the garden we stumbled upon when we first came to town."

Sam grinned. "God plants His Garden wherever weary souls need to rest. Do you remember the story in Scripture where Jesus' disciples came back from a mission exhausted but excited to tell about it and Jesus said to them, 'come away with me to a quiet place and rest awhile?' I often imagine he took them to a place such as this. It never ceases to amaze me how many people miss these beautiful sanctuaries. There would be a lot less stress in people's lives if they took time to enjoy Sabbath. It's where true healing is."

James ran back to Matthew, wide-eyed and breathless with excitement, "I found a cave, Matt. It's huge! Come and see!"

Matthew looked puzzled, "I thought there were only two caves, Sam. We passed them both on the way up here."

Sam nodded. "There is indeed a third cave that the townspeople aren't aware of because they think that the trail ends at the second cave. I spent hours here in my youth, especially when I needed solitude to hear God's direction for my life." Sam spread his arms wide and turned around. "Isn't this a magnificent place? I couldn't wait to share it with you."

Joseph agreed. "It is beautiful here. Is this where you are going to tell us about how this mountain became sacred?"

Sam beamed. "Indeed it is but, first, let us prepare our picnic. Matthew and James, will you two gather some of those plump and juicy berries, while Joseph and I spread out a blanket near the waterfall? It's a marvelous spot. My favorite in all the world. There is even a place where you can sit and see the whole cabin grounds. The waterfall is beautiful and feeds the stream below that we crossed over."

Joseph stood with his hands on his hips, gazing at the trees and bushes. "I am amazed that all this fruit is ripe already."

"God's Garden is always in bloom, my friends. And only those who look with their inside eyes can see it."

Sam opened a pouch attached to a belt around his waist and pulled out a plastic bag. Handing it to Matthew and James, he said with a twinkle in his eyes, "Go and gather God's banquet. Pick whatever looks good to you and meet us at the waterfall. You can't miss us. We'll be the only ones there."

As Matthew and James ran over to the fruit trees and berry bushes, Sam and Joseph strolled over to the cave.

"Where are we going to get a blanket to spread out here, Sam? Your pouch doesn't look big enough carry one."

Sam threw his head back and laughed. "Wouldn't you be shocked if I did pull one out. But it just so happens that we already have a blanket up here. It's one I always used when I came here to pray. A quilt, actually, that my mother made. I carved out a cubbyhole in the cave wall to keep it in so that I wouldn't have to carry it every time."

Joseph followed Sam into the cave entrance, and turning to his right, Sam removed a rock cover and pulled out his quilt. Then replacing the rock, they left the cave and turned toward the waterfall. Walking around the perimeter of the cave they moved behind the waterfall to a small grassy clearing of lush grass covered with blue, purple, and pink wildflowers. Joseph couldn't believe his eyes, "This spot makes a perfect fort, Sam. We could hide here and still see everything below us. It's incredible."

"I'm pleased you like it and I am honored to share it with you and your brothers."

Sam and Joseph turned to the sound of laughter and cheering. James came hopping and skipping around the cave and across the grass, followed by Matthew, who was carrying the bag filled with fruit."

"That was fun," said James. "Wait till you see what we picked. The berries are huge."

Sam chuckled at James' excitement. "Now we can have a banquet. Each of you grab a corner of the blanket and let's spread it out."

They removed their shoes and gathered in the center of the blanket. Sam said, "Joseph, the third parent, if you will graciously allow me, I would like to take your place for the moment and lead us in prayer.

117

Joseph nodded his assent and Sam began, "Abba, dear Abba, thank you for this beautiful day and for my new friends, Joseph, the third parent, Reverend Valente, and James the Great, whom you have created in your image and likeness. Bless them abundantly and fill their lives with a sense of Divine Purpose. May they always be surrounded by people who will be living examples of Your Love. Help them be successful in finding a home together. Guide them over every obstacle and may their journey in this life lead only to you, their true friend, their Abba. I ask you to bless our feast. May it nourish us body and soul."

Joseph, Matthew, and James responded, "Amen."

Sam opened his pouch again, and removing a small loaf of bread, raised it up and closed his eyes in silent prayer. Then breaking the bread, he passed it to his friends saying, "Take and eat, and be nourished for the Journey."

As each boy received the bread, Sam became transfigured before them, and his garments became dazzling, his eyes radiant, light shining through every pore of his body. Joseph, Matthew, and James, as they consumed the bread, also became radiant. And the whole land about them shimmered and they were again lost in their surroundings, transfused with heavenly grace, lifted beyond the visible, beyond the veil, to the New Jerusalem.

And there was music and dancing, marvelous white beings of light swayed and twirled and danced with merriment and abandon and unashamed joy. They joined the dance, losing themselves in playful exuberance, laughing, unburdened by the weight of their bodies, unencumbered, reaching out to each other in joy and delight.

And there was another boy with them, reaching out to James. James saw him rise out of his paralyzed body and join the dance. He took his hand and knew the boy's name was Rick, but he didn't know how he knew. They danced and laughed. Rick told James, in melody, not to fear, to trust God in every circumstance, to always listen for the music inside him, and then he was gone, but not their friendship.

Then the radiance began to diminish, gradually and gently. The swirling dance of the angels slowed, the music faded. The boys found themselves reclining on the blanket with Sam leaning over them, rousing them to wakefulness, "Come on, sleepyheads, naptime is over. I have a story to tell."

Joseph, Matthew, and James sat up, rubbing their eyes and stretching. Matthew said, "I just had a dream that we were in Heaven."

James said, excitedly, "I did too, and we were dancing with angels! And I met a boy my age named Rick."

Joseph said, "So did I. It's more like a memory than a dream."

Some of Sam's radiance had remained. Staring out over the mountain, he said, "Abba's Garden is full of surprises, and this mountain, in particular, is sacred. If you boys are not too tired, I would like to tell you how that came to be."

"Tell us, Sam. I can't wait any longer to hear your story," said Joseph.

119

Sam began, "In the early 1800's, a group native to this land settled in this place now called The Diamond Lake Cabin Colony. They were new converts to the Christian faith and had fled their homeland because of persecution. It was their desire to imitate as closely as possible the life described in Holy Scriptures, while still respecting the culture and traditions of their people. They also befriended the villagers who lived nearby. The villagers helped them to get settled, sharing their food and resources, because when the group fled their homeland, they took nothing with them. They developed into a faith-filled community much the same as when the church first began, and lived in peace for many years before they disappeared."

"What happened to them?" asked James.

"Did they all disappear at the same time?" asked Matthew.

"There are a couple of stories that circulated among the villagers. One is that warriors from their tribe found them and forced them to go back to their clan. Another story that has evidence to back it up is that one of the families in the village, who was intolerant of the Indians, chased them off the land by showing them a phony deed of ownership."

"Why didn't they fight them for it?" James asked.

"Because," said Sam, "they had chosen a life of nonviolence in accord with Holy Scriptures, and in prayer, discerned that God was calling them to move. And because they didn't know that the deed was a forgery. Honest people can sometimes be easily deceived because they believe all people are sincere like they are."

"How did they make this mountain sacred, Sam? Was it because they wouldn't use weapons?" asked Joseph.

"Yes, Joseph, and even more. There is another story that spread around the village about a healing that took place, I believe, on the very spot where Reverend Valente fell. It has been handed down that a young Indian maiden was brought back to life from a knife wound, healed, in fact, by her brother."

Sam smiled at Joseph. "It happened when her brothers decided not to execute the man from the village who threw the knife. He was secretly in love with her and was following the tribe up the mountain. He threw the knife hoping they would think he was a warrior and tough enough to become one of them, but it lodged in the maiden's neck."

"Why did he throw a knife at her if he was in love with her," asked James.

"He wasn't aiming at her, but at a tree. He just wanted to get the chief's attention. It happened when the tribe was climbing up this mountain to hide a manuscript for their descendants to find."

Joseph asked, "What happened to the young man?"

"According to the story that is believed by many to be true, he joined the tribe. They adopted him, and in gratitude to God for saving the woman's life, he converted to Christianity and adopted their way of life. His family knew he wanted to join the tribe and so they wrote the phony deed. They were hoping that he would come to his senses once the Indians were gone."

"I guess he did come to his senses."

Sam answered him, "That he did, Joseph. His life among the tribe made Abba very proud. He thrived in way that never would have been possible with his family."

Matthew asked, "Where is the manuscript?"

Sam continued, "So far it has never been found. But the tribe left behind a message to the villagers before they vanished thanking them for their kindness and friendship, and promising to keep them in their prayers. In the letter, they alluded to the manuscript that they hid for a time yet to come."

"What does that mean, Sam?" asked James.

"It means, little brother," laughed Matthew, "that it will take forever to find, and maybe never."

"Well, there is a better chance than never," said Sam, "because in the Catholic Church in town there is a deacon who is a direct descendant and who has been studying the history of his people. At the Youth Rally that is taking place on these grounds today, Deacon John Salerno will be inviting the young people of the town to join him in a special project, a search of this mountain over the summer. He will probably get a lot of interested helpers."

"Maybe we can help," said Matthew. "It sounds like fun."

"Don't forget why we're here, Matt," Joseph reminded him. "We can't risk being seen by the police."

"You're right, but maybe we can conduct our own search. We can start up here. Nobody will find us up here. And if they do manage to come this far there are plenty of places to hide."

"And you can see so far from up here," said James. "We will be able to see anyone who is coming up."

"And did you notice the rainbow? I've never seen one so big or brilliant, and you can look right through it and still see everything below us," said Matthew, the awe apparent in his voice.

"The ever-present sign of God's covenant with all people," said Sam beaming. "It is another reason why I loved this spot in particular."

For a while Sam and the boys just sat gazing out over the cabin grounds, listening to the melody of life around them, breathing in the scent of the fresh flowers, immersing themselves in the beauty of their surroundings. The countryside, as far as they could see, was indeed magnificent. And, along with the delicious aromas wafting on the breeze from the cooking fires below, they could hear laughter and music. Sam broke their musing.

"Now that you know the Way, feel free to come up here anytime. It is a great place just to sit and think … and pray. I spent countless hours here, my own heaven on earth. I don't think anyone has ever found the path that leads up here, but now you know it."

James looked up at Sam, a troubled look crossing his brow. "You're not going away, Sam, are you?" he asked, panic edging into his voice.

Sam pulled James onto his lap and embraced him. "I'll be around whenever I can. I never abandon my friends. But I do live many miles from here and have a business to run. Don't worry, though. My mother can always get in touch with me, and I don't think she'll let any of you out of her sight. I do believe she has a short leash and knows how to wield it," he added with a grin.

James leaned back against Sam, and asked, "What work do you do in your business?"

"I am a carpenter by trade but the business has grown so much that I find myself more involved with paperwork than woodworking. I miss the actual feel of the wood in my hands and contact with my patrons. I used to love inviting them back to the workshop to have coffee and chat while I worked on their orders. It was how I got to know them. I'd listen to stories, and they loved the wisdom I shared with them and we'd become friends. But now I spend too much time in the office doing paperwork instead of enjoying the touch of the wood." Sam threw his head back and laughed. "Do you want to know what I really miss the most? The expressions on people's faces as they watched a figure emerge from the wood. It would tickle them somewhere deep inside to see a form take shape," Sam winked at them and grinned. "It was like witnessing life from death."

Matthew teased Sam, "Paper is a form of wood, Sam. You could make paper dolls, paper fans, paper planes…"

Sam chuckled. "And, if I am not mistaken, wood is a four-letter word. Isn't that correct, Reverend Valente?"

Joseph groaned, "Oh, no! Here it comes."

Matthew stood up, spread his arms wide, and bellowed, "Wood is indeed a four-letter word, created by God for the express purpose of carving important things

124

like baseball bats and playgrounds. Any other use of this God-given natural resource is fraudulent and punishable by hard time in Gehenna."

Joseph grabbed Matthew by the seat of his pants and pulled him back down.

Sam ruffled Matthew's hair and said, "I like the way you think, Reverend. If you were in charge of the whole world it would indeed become one magnificent park, also a four-letter word. What a great idea! And you've convinced me of something I've been considering. I'll hire an accountant to handle the paperwork and move myself back into the workshop closer to the reason why I went into business in the first place, my people."

Joseph groaned. "Don't encourage him, Sam. The Reverend's head is already too big to live with. Could we come and see your woodshop sometime?"

"I would love to have you come and visit me," answered Sam, "but wait until you are settled where Abba is calling you. Do not take any unnecessary risks. And now, before we return to the cabin, allow me to bless you in this sacred place with the words Mom always blessed me with before any import task."

Joseph, Matthew, and James bowed their heads and Sam prayed, using the words of Saint Paul to the Ephesians, "Out of His infinite glory, may He give you power through His Spirit for your hidden self to grow strong, so that Christ may live in your hearts through faith, and then, planted in love and built on love, you will with all the saints have strength to grasp the breadth and the length, the height and the depth; until, knowing the love of Christ, which is beyond all knowledge, you are filled with the utter fullness of God."

Then Sam reached out to form the Sign of the Cross on their foreheads … and reaching out to Rick in spirit, touched him with healing, bringing strength to his little legs, he was going to need it …

****

Rick was indeed tuned in to another world. He could now see the white angelic beings whom he could only sense before. And he wasn't sure if seeing was the right word, because the scene was the same whether his eyes were opened or closed. The beautiful angelic beings were stationed around the room giving respectful attention to Deacon John Salerno.

****

And the lady with the beautiful voice was singing in his heart, telling him to remain still, for Rick knew something had changed. "Your legs are better, but they are not strong enough to stand on yet."

Rick said to her in his heart, "But I can feel tingling in my legs, and I can wiggle my toes."

And the musical voice answered him, "Your muscles are still very weak, but they will get stronger. You just have to be patient."

Rick answered, his head bowed, his eyes closed, "I danced on the mountain. Did you see? Were you there? There was a picnic up there, too. And music. And angels were dancing. And I met a boy my age. I think his name is James, and even though he was dancing, he was sad. I could feel it in his heart. He is also afraid, but he won't tell anyone."

The voice continued to sing to Rick, to help him stay calm, he was so excited; he could wiggle his toes. She sang to Rick, "Yes, I was on the mountain with you. You dance beautifully, but you must be patient. Keep resting so you can get stronger. James is going to need your help. You are correct. He is sad and afraid, and so are his brothers. But my Son is up there too and is helping. Did you see Him?"

Rick answered, "Yes, I saw a man on the mountain. He was dancing too and was having so much fun. And He was so full of light that he made everything glow."

The beautiful voice spoke with obvious pleasure, "God's Garden is always radiant with love, peace, and joy to help weary souls find nourishment and rest for the journey. Those boys need to get stronger too, but James is going to need your friendship and support in a special way soon. He is six years old just like you. Will you be his friend?"

Rick answered, a melody forming in his heart, "Yes, I will be happy to be his friend, and help him. Can I tell Nick that I can wiggle my toes?"

"Yes, tell him, but not until after you return to your home. You both worked so hard today at the rally. I am so proud of you both. Tell Nick, but let him know that you will still need his help. Remind him that he helped you

get better by always being there for you. Thank him for all he has done for you."

"If I help James, will I still be able to help my brother?"

"You have already helped Nick more than you know. By agreeing to come back and submitting to his vigilance toward you, his heart has been molded, and he is now better able to resist the pull of the gang. He is not aware of it yet, but when the time is right, he will be. Thank you, Rick, for your hard work on behalf of your beautiful brother."

"You are welcome. Thank you for being our friend."

As the room broke into thunderous applause, Rick came back to the present, and joined in the applause. This had been the best day ever …

CHAPTER 8

King Without A Kingdom

Logan parked his motorcycle up the road from the main entrance of the Diamond Lake Cabin Colony and watched the caravan of cars and vans leave. As far as he was concerned this had been the worst day ever. No one had shown up at the meeting place at the appointed time. And Nick ... Logan was seething with anger. Nick was supposed to have left Rick home. Instead, he had taken him to the rally and then had the nerve to spend the day taking care of the little brat. He was going to have to do something about that. Even the other two recruits hovered around Rick. The little twerp seemed to have a magnetic personality that Logan couldn't comprehend. At any rate, they were going to have to decide in which court they were going to play ball.

But Logan was also concerned ... and, he hated to admit it, scared. He didn't want to give them a choice. He didn't think the new recruits were bright enough to come up with the right answer. They certainly didn't come up with any more recruits. What jerks! Right now Logan only seemed to be in charge of an anthill, minus the ants, they probably wouldn't cooperate either. Come to think of it, neither would the dirt ... if he wasn't in such a bad mood, he might even be able to find some humor in it.

He was still determined to win a stronghold in this quiet, boring little hamlet. It was the perfect setting for his headquarters and he wasn't going to give up on it too easily … not until he won the big seat, that is. He wasn't going to let these simpletons ruin his dreams.

And what about that Baptist minister, the Reverend Scarecrow, with his candle ministry? Instead of running away next time, Logan decided he would just stand up to him and blow out his stupid candle. But those eyes! Those deep, penetrating, blue eyes haunted his dreams. Why were they so familiar? With the Reverend's long, shiny black hair and his motorcycle garb, his perfectly straight white teeth, and his firm jaw, why were his eyes so prominent? And it wasn't just that those eyes were so familiar to him, those eyes also held recognition in them, like they knew him, Logan. But from where? The last time he really looked into eyes that bore into him so deeply was six years ago, as he straddled a classmate, had him pinned to the ground, held a rock over his head, and brought it down. The look in those eyes never wavered, never pleaded, never feared. But that scrawny, pimple-faced geek bore no resemblance to the Reverend Scarecrow … except for those eyes.

Logan watched the end of the caravan leave the cabin ground and wondered what his next move should be. If he chased down the recruits and confronted them, he would either look too eager … or too pathetic, and he would lose the tenuous control he had over them. It would be better for him to chalk this one up as a loss for now. He waited until the cars and vans were out of sight, then started up his motorcycle and took off, leaving town by the back roads.

****

130

After finishing their search of the grounds around Gilead, Officer Bill Bennett had the police officers return to the rally. Since the day was getting late, he expected the boys to blend in with the town's youth to get food. Leo had requested permission to remain hidden on the cabin grounds where he had been when he first observed the boys crossing the footbridge. He wasn't going to let them away this time. Bill allowed him to remain and had taken Ralph back to the rally to watch the tables where food was being served. They would have a better chance of catching the boys if he kept Leo and Ralph apart.

Later, back at the station, he would help them deal with the tension that existed between them. He had a natural talent for conflict resolution, a remarkable ability to restore friendships between people, mainly because he could discern when the time was right. Leo and Ralph were both good men and good police officers who had not intended to hurt each other. And he also knew that the tension existed because, deep down, they cared for one another; and when they reached the point where they could voice it they would be able to forgive each other and move on … together. He sensed the time had arrived.

****

Sam and the boys reached the footbridge. Sam and Matthew walked across on their hands, James hopped across, and Joseph stopped in the middle, pausing, lost in thought, staring at the shelter that had been their first hideout. They had arrived only yesterday, experiencing their first wave of victory. So much had happened ... more than they had planned. And the part they didn't plan was like a gift from God.

Joseph prayed in the quiet of his heart, thanking God for their beautiful day, for Sam and Martha, for his brothers' ready cooperation, trusting him to lead them home. Truth be told, he was feeling his confidence slip away. Panic was creeping in like an uninvited guest. Everything had seemed so simple yesterday, their plan, their determination to succeed, as if they would be able to run away and just step into their new home. He didn't know what their next step should be but he couldn't get over the feeling they were being guided and even carried in their distress. And, why not? They had always been taught to trust God, to pray in need and in gratitude. But the help from God had never been so tangible before.

Joseph continued to pray in need and in gratitude as he watched Sam and his brothers play. "Please, Abba, don't let them break us up. I couldn't stand not living with my brothers. They're all I have in the world right now. All I need. Even if we live in a mud hole, it would be fine with me, and I know, with them, too; just as long as we are together ... Please, God ... what do we do now?"

Joseph fought hard to hold back his tears. It had been such a beautiful day...

His silent scream reached the tender heart of Sam, who reached out in spirit to embrace Joseph, to reassure him, "Let not you heart be troubled, my son. Trust in God and trust in me. I've come to prepare a place for you. Do not let circumstances discourage you. You and

132

your dear brothers have chosen the better path, and you shall not be deprived."

Joseph felt his fear lift, replaced by renewed confidence and a sense of peace. He knew his brothers were as determined as he was to succeed. It didn't matter what obstacle they ran up against, they would conquer it.

Joseph's fear had also been replaced by a cheerfulness that took him by surprise. The festive mood had returned. It was as if a dark cloud had collided with him and then dashed off.

****

The angelic curtain ministry was also having fun ... way too much fun. Veiling the scene was one thing, but every once in a while, Sam had to remind them not to get carried away. Think inside the cloud. They didn't need fireworks, wild horses, or trumpets. Thunder and lightning were only permitted to get people moving in the right direction, or to create delays that would allow the innocent to escape. And, above all, nothing too bizarre. The created scene had to appear natural. Just help us return to the cabin undetected, Sam reminded them, we don't need the choir right now.

****

Martha sat in a rocking chair on the front porch reading and enjoying her surroundings, while Moses lay at her feet chewing on a bone. Dinner was ready and she couldn't wait to hear about their day. Even though she already knew, it would be better to hear about it from the boys themselves. They would each have their own story to tell, their own unique perspectives.

Moses dropped his bone and lifted his head, suddenly alert. As quickly as a jackrabbit running from a fox, he darted off the porch, racing around the cabin toward the footbridge, barking excitedly. Martha put down her book and stood up. They were back. She was as eager to see them as Moses and would have liked to race over to greet them, but she had to make sure everything was ready. Instead she turned and opened the door to the cabin, and upon entering, looked at the table she had set for dinner. What a wondrous sight would greet their eyes. And the food would be as delicious, a real celebration. She hadn't started out to make a feast. When Sam had teased her about cooking while she kept the home fires burning, she had planned to make another pot of soup and bake more bread. She wanted the cabin to smell good when they came back, so they would feel comfortable, ready to sit and tell about their day with Sam … and perhaps spend another night.

Martha had gone into town intending to purchase ingredients for soup, but changed her plan as she watched the butcher place fresh turkeys on display in the meat case. She chose a small turkey and placed it in her shopping cart, and also picked everything else necessary to prepare a real Thanksgiving feast. As her idea grew, so did the number of items in her shopping cart. She even remembered whipped cream for the pumpkin pie.

Now everything was ready for a delicious dinner. Martha's best white lace tablecloth covered the table. Ivory candlesticks that held tapered gold candles were placed at each side of a floral centerpiece filled with a variety of fresh-cut flowers. At the head of each place setting stood a pastel, multihued, lace napkin folded inside a napkin ring. On each side of gold-trimmed, white plates inlaid with a gold snowflake design lay delicate silverware polished to the peak of brilliance. A plentiful breadbasket filled with a variety of homemade rolls was placed at one end of the table, and a crystal dish filled with homemade cranberry relish was placed at the other end. Martha stood gazing at her beautiful handiwork, her hands folded under her chin, her heart beating to the tune of her excitement. It had been a beautiful day, and it wasn't over yet.

The sound of footsteps on the porch and the turning of the doorknob ended Martha's musing for the moment. The celebration was about to begin.

Moses came through the door first, quickly followed by James yelling, "Martha, Martha! We're home."

Moses turned back to the door, barking at them to hurry in. James stopped dead in his tracks, staring at the table, wide-eyed, his mouth wide open, the look of a young child standing in front of a huge pile of presents.

The entrance was repeated as they each came through the door. They stood there speechless, gaping, and bright-eyed, at the unexpected festive scene before them.

Sam was the first to speak, "Is God coming to dinner, Mom?"

Martha grinned. "You'll find out after you get washed up. Come on, now. Get moving, so you can come to the table. I've been waiting forever."

As Sam and the boys headed toward the bathroom, Martha could hear Matthew say, "Soap is a four-letter word, you know."

She chuckled to herself as she walked over to the oven to put more of the food dishes on the table. Matthew's humor was always on the tip of his tongue and his mind and heart were always close to God. His charming personality and playful nature drew friends to him, and instead of making fun of him for going to church, they went because of him. He'd make a great priest someday. Young people were drawn to him because he knew how to combine play and prayer in holy festivity. Martha also perceived that he and his brothers were troubled over having missed Mass, for it was Sunday. When they sat in front of the fireplace after dinner, she knew that Sam would console them.

James came skipping up the hallway, past the fireplace, and stopped in front of the table, the glow on his face brighter than the glare of sunlight through a polished window. Joseph and Matthew also returned and stood on each side of James, staring in wonder and awe. Sam walked over to the kitchen counter, lifted the platter of turkey, and carried it over to the table. Smiling at the boys he said, "It appears, as expected for someone of such noble heart, that Mom has prepared us a magnificent feast. Let us gather round the table and enjoy it. Joseph the third parent, will you please take your place at the head of the table and lead us in a prayer of gratitude?"

Joseph moved, as if in a dream, to one end of the table and discovered an ivory napkin ring that had his name engraved on the face of it in delicately formed script.

Beneath it was engraved in the same delicate lettering, 'Come to the Banquet'. Matthew and James took their places at each side of Joseph and discovered a napkin ring with their name engraved with the same message in the same delicate lettering.

Sam placed the platter of turkey on the table and took his place next to Matthew, while Martha took her place next to James. Noticing that there was still one more place set at the opposite end of the table from Joseph, James asked, "Who else is coming?"

Martha, beaming at them all, bowed her head and answered, "God is indeed invited, and is already here among us. I always set a place for Abba at every feast to remind me that, just as we are welcome at the Heavenly Banquet, so God is always welcome at my table."

Joseph responded, "I like your idea, Martha. I like it a lot. When my brothers and I are settled back in our home, we will do the same thing. If our plan works, I will set a place for God every day to show my gratitude."

"If?" Sam chimed in, "If? My friend, you were right the first time. WHEN you and your brothers are settled. And now, will you please begin your new tradition by lighting the candles and leading us in a prayer of thanksgiving?"

Joseph lit the candles, then paused for a moment before continuing, "Thank you, Abba, for this glorious day spent on the mountain with our friend, Sam. Bless him as generously as being in his presence has blessed us today. Bless Martha for preparing this wonderful feast for us and for taking us in and making us feel welcome and safe. Please guide us in our plans so that my brothers and I will be able to stay together. Please guide all the people involved so that they will understand how important that is for us. Please, Abba…"

Joseph's voice cracked and a tear escaped down his cheek. And, as before, the plea was met by Sam as he reached out to Joseph, tender heart to wounded heart, and answered, using His words as recorded by the prophet Isaiah, 'Fear not, I am with you; be not dismayed; I am your God. I will strengthen you, and help you, and uphold you with my right hand of justice.'

And, again, Joseph's spirit was lifted, his fear dispelled. He looked up, reassured and smiling, and upon opening out his hands, everyone responded, "Amen."

James added, licking his lips, "And thank you for this wonderful food."

Sam's booming laughter bubbled up like a fountain as he reached over and placed the platter of turkey in front of him. Then rising to his feet, he began to go through the motions of stretching and flexing his muscles. Martha just grinned at him, then turned to the boys and said, "While my son prepares himself for the challenge of slicing the turkey, tell me all about your day. And don't leave anything out. I want to hear it all."

Inside the cabin, the boys began to fill Martha in as Sam sliced the turkey. The yummy smells and joyful laughter reached every corner of the cabin; the cozy glow of the fire in the fireplace reached out to envelope them in warmth and light.

The smoke from the chimney merged with the song of the angelic host and rose to greet the heavens.

****

Outside, the sun was beginning to set and the two policemen stationed at the doors of the deserted cabin were getting impatient. A strong wind was blowing in from the west bringing more dark clouds. Calling to Officer Bill Bennett on his radio, Mark said, "There's no sign of the boys, Bill. They must have moved on."

Bill responded, "Keep your positions for now. Leo hasn't seen them leave by the hiker's entrance, so they are probably still around."

Grumbling to himself, Mark put his radio back in its pouch and pulled his hood up over his head. It had started raining again.

****

Nick tucked his brother in front of him on his bike and quickly pedaled away ahead of everyone, leaving by the front entrance. He couldn't leave by the back entrance, as he usually did, in case Logan was there. He was supposed to be meeting with him at their deserted cabin with Tony and Frank and some new recruits, but he had gotten lost in the spirit of the rally and had helped more than he intended. And he didn't want to bring Rick to the meetings anymore. Logan was displaying more and more hostility toward Rick and it was beginning to scare him. Even more, the idea of joining the Jaguars no longer enticed him. He couldn't understand why either, but he no longer felt like he belonged. He had been so eager to prove it, to show how tough he was. All he wanted to do now was get Rick home safe, then sit down, and do some serious thinking. He was so confused.

And Rick was different. Nick could not quite put his finger on it, but Rick seemed lighter, as if he was carrying some of his own weight. When Nick had lifted him onto his back to carry him to a bench outside while he went to get his bike, he had felt some tightening in Rick's leg muscles. *Was it a spasm or was he getting stronger?* He would certainly have to check it out when he got him home. Nick prayed in the silence of his heart, "Please, Lord, let it be true. Help Rick get better. Help him walk again. I'll do anything you want, just help him …" Nick's eyes filled with tears and he fought back the urge to cry. After all this time, he couldn't stand it if Rick was getting worse.

But Sam heard the cry of Nick's heart and responded, reaching out, at the same moment, to two wounded hearts with one message of consolation, 'Fear not, I am with you; be not dismayed; I am your God. I will strengthen you, and help you, and uphold you with my right hand of justice.'

Even though Nick could not yet hear God's Word in his heart, he still was able to receive some of the comfort the Word provided, for his heart was indeed softer than before and less cluttered. Pedaling faster than he ever had in his life, he left the cabin colony. He couldn't wait to get Rick home. And he had never been happier that he hadn't told Logan where he lived. They were safe for now. Even Tony and Frank had skipped the meeting and were on their way home. They would have to explain themselves to Logan later … maybe.

****

After Deacon John made sure the girls were buckled in, he climbed behind the wheel of his jeep and started it up. Following the caravan to the main road of the cabin colony, he separated from the line and headed toward the resident's cabins.

John had never felt so energized. Though quiet and shy by nature, all he wanted to do now was cheer and dance. The youth's response to his proposal filled him with hope.

The people of Hillcrest had done so much to make him feel welcome. God bless them all! Now they were ready to help him fulfill the desire of his heart and help him search for the manuscript. His dream could not come true without their help. Even the parents volunteered. How could he say no? All his life he had faced rejection and ridicule because of his heritage. People had even gone so far as to fear him. He couldn't fight the masses or argue constantly with them about what his people were really like. It would have been easier to pass a law banning the television shows that portrayed Native Indians in such a bad light. Since the chance of that happening was nil, he had just faded into the background, keeping to himself. Far from becoming lonely and bitter, however, his quiet life had paved the way for him to develop a close relationship with God. And God had brought him to Hillcrest, to these wonderful people. God bless them all! Fortunately, he didn't have far to drive. Mary Anne's cabin was just up the road.

As John pulled up the driveway, Jessica and Bernadette were already rolling down the windows and calling to their grandmother, "Nana! Nana! We're back! Jumping out of the jeep as soon as John stopped they ran to Mary Anne, covering her with hugs and kisses.

"I'm thrilled you girls are back too. How was your day?"

"We had the most fun ever, Nana! I wish it didn't have to end," said Jessica.

"And Deacon John told us about a special project for the summer that will be a lot of fun. Mom, can we stay with Nana and be part of it?" Bernadette pleaded.

"That depends," said Mary Anne, winking at Teresa, "you girls don't mean to imply that I'll be playing second fiddle to your fun project?"

Bernadette leaned her head on her grandmother. "Oh, Nana! You know we love you best! Please? Can we stay with you this summer?"

"We'll help you in the bakery in our spare time." Jessica added. "Please?"

Mary Anne laughed and held both girls close, "Of course you can stay, if it's okay with your mother, that is. It'll be a joy to have the both of you for the summer."

Rocco looked at Teresa, and said, with a twinkle in his eye. "Maybe you can stay too, Teresa, since the lease is up on your apartment. Stay with your Mom until you decide where you're going to move. Maybe it'll even be around here."

John overheard Teresa's response as he joined the group. "You could even find a teaching job in town until our new school is built. We'd love to have you on the planning committee, Teresa. With your experience traveling and teaching in various places, you'd be a valuable asset to the development of a faith-based curriculum."

Teresa found herself surrounded, all eyes on her, and even though Rocco was smiling, his eyes were pleading, 'I need you to stay! Please!'

How could she say no? "Tell me more about the new school. When are you going to start building it?"

"Sounds like a good time for coffee and pie." Mary Anne said, "Let's go up to the deck, and John, you can fill us in." She winked at him and said, "You do have time to fill us in, don't you?"

"Wild horses couldn't drag me away right now, Mare. Thank you for the invite," he said, his expression brighter than the white paint that still adorned his face.

As the group walked to the deck, they heard another car pull up the driveway. John said, "Luke and Maddie are here. I think we're going to need more pie. Good thing you own a bakery, Mare."

Mary Anne laughed. "Good thing, John. The more, the merrier. You get ready to tell your story. Jake and I will get the party going."

Jake had just stepped through the back door and heard Mary Anne. He stuck out his lower lip and said, "You wouldn't be talking about another whole boat-load of dishes. My delicate fingers are already wrinkled from having been in water forever." Jake held up his hands to show everyone.

Rocco held his hands next to Jake's. "Uncle Jake, I've NEVER, seen your hands so clean. Maybe you should wash dishes forever more often."

Jake looked at him in feigned offense, putting a hand to his heart. "Rocco, I have a reputation in this town. If God had meant for us mechanics to have clean hands, he wouldn't have made grease to stick."

Mary Anne put her arm around Jake, and said, "Just for you, Jake, we'll use paper plates and plastic forks."

As they reached the deck, Jake could be heard saying, "Now yer talkin', Mare."

Jessica and Bernadette ran up the driveway to greet Father Luke and Sister Madeleine, both of them talking at once, "We're staying for the summer! Nana said it was okay! We're going to help search for the manuscript!"

Both girls were jumping up and down and clapping their hands in excitement. They were joined in their celebration by Sister Madeleine. "I am delighted to hear it. That is why Luke and I came back here. We wanted to make sure you felt welcome to join us. Oh! We are going to have such fun!"

Deacon John watched them from the top of the driveway. He was excited enough to join in the dance, but it wouldn't have looked right. It was definitely a girl thing. Later on, before he retired for the evening, he would go for a run … and thank God.

****

Nick pedaled up the driveway and pulled into the storage shed his father had built. He had dubbed it the Leaning Tower of Shed because it tilted to one side, as if threatening to fall over. But today he laughed. *'Go ahead,' he thought, 'fall as many times as you want. Rick has already made my day, and Dad will just build you again.'*

Elaine Farrell opened the back door and greeted her sons, "Hi, boys. Glad you're back. It's been way too quiet around here. How was the rally?"

Nick knew his mother was relieved he had decided to go to the rally. She had been worried about her son's attraction to the gang. He had heard her praying when she thought he was sleeping. And their new pastor had helped. The Reverend Gregory Marshall had paid a visit to personally invite Nick, and had encouraged him to bring his little brother. Greg had promised Nick that he would help so he wouldn't have to worry about him.

Nick brought his bike to a stop inside the shed and came out, carrying Rick on his back. "Hi, Mom!" he said. "We had a great time, the most fun ever."

Nick could feel Rick resting his chin on his shoulder, and knew he was probably tuned in to music in his heart again. It didn't bother him this time, because he thought he could feel Rick's legs clinging to his sides as he carried him. Excitement began to well up within him but he was still afraid it was wishful thinking. But he wouldn't imagine it, would he?

Elaine held the door open for her sons and said to them as they passed by her, "There are some warm cookies on a plate. Sit at the table and tell me all about your day."

Nick carefully set his brother down on a chair and then knelt down in front of him. He usually carried Rick in his arms into the house, but he wanted to see if he could indeed feel Rick's leg muscles tighten. *Had it just been a figment of his imagination, desire gone mad, or was it for real? And did Rick notice? He hadn't said anything. You'd think that he'd be the first to notice.* But he just sat in the chair and reached for a cookie … and flexed his foot.

"Mom!" Nick screamed, jumping to his feet, then falling back down to his knees. He put his hands around Rick's legs … and felt his calf muscles tighten.

"Mom!" he screamed again, jumping to his feet, jumping up and down, his hands on each side of his head, his eyes filling with tears. "Mom! Rick has feeling in his legs! Rick can move his legs! Rick, you can move your legs! Mom!"

Nick spun around and then knelt in front of his brother, again putting his hands around Rick's legs.

Rick flexed his foot … and reached for another cookie. Elaine came running over and knelt in front of her son, holding his feet in her hands, the expression on her face a mixture of astonishment and hope.

"Baby, is it true?" she whispered, too stunned to raise her voice, too afraid to awaken. *'Oh, God! If this is a dream, please let this night last forever!'*

The lady with the beautiful voice was singing to Rick. "Keep calm," her melodic voice guided, "let your mother and brother enjoy their discovery. They have been praying so hard."

Rick took another bite of cookie … and wiggled his toes. The cookies were still warm, his favorite kind.

Elaine put her hands around Rick's legs and felt the movement, and her ecstatic scream of joy burst through the walls and roof of the house, rising to join with the music of the angels, blending to form a song of victory, of triumph, of joy … of joy. The shouting reached the ears of her husband who had been out working in the field, getting it ready for planting. Brian jumped off his tractor and ran back to the house as fast as he could. Bursting through the back door, he stopped abruptly, as if colliding with an invisible wall.

The scene that met his eyes was far different from what he expected. Elaine, Nick and Rick were locked in tight embrace, laughing and crying. Nick had tried to back away so his mother could get closer to Rick, but Elaine had pulled him back in and hugged them both, telling Nick he was an important part of the miracle.

"You never knew it, Nick, but I watched you pray over Rick every night. And you took such good care of him. God healed him through you, I know it. Thank you for all your hard work, my beautiful son. This wouldn't have happened without you. You never gave up believing your brother would get better, did you." She hugged him tighter.

Nick cried then. He could hold the floodgates back no longer. Rick was better. It was true. Their father joined the excitement. He reached for Rick, lifted him high above his head, and studied his legs. Then he sat on the chair and put Rick on his lap, and hugging him tightly, threw his head back, rocking and crying.

Nick remembered their promise to phone Dr. Matthews. It was Sunday evening, but that didn't matter because he had given them his home number. He wanted to be called immediately in the event of any change. He had made them promise to call.

"Forget office hours," he had said to them in the waiting room. "If Rick gets feeling back in his legs, you're going to want to scream the news, and I won't want to wait to hear about it. After you, I want to be the first to know. So call. I don't care when. You're not leaving until you promise. Go ahead, promise."

They had promised to call no matter the day or hour. Nick had sensed that day that Dr. Matthews expected Rick to recover, and he knew he would be praying for him.

Elaine made the call. The next phone call was to Reverend Gregory Marshall. He had been a regular visitor at their home ever since his arrival in town, encouraging Nick to keep active in youth ministry and away from the gang. She finally reached him on his cell phone, "Greg, can you come over? Rick's legs ... you're not gonna believe ... this is incredible ... can you come now?"

Greg answered, "Now suits me just fine, Elaine."

Elaine turned then and saw Greg standing at the back door, his cell phone next to his ear, holding his helmet under his other arm. In their excitement, they never heard his motorcycle roll up the driveway.

****

Greg entered, leaving his helmet on the floor by the back door, and joined the celebration. During the meeting at the community hall, he had observed a subtle

148

shift in Rick's posture as he sat on his brother's lap. When Nick carried him out of the meeting hall, he noticed that Rick held himself a little higher on Nick's back. And now his observation was confirmed, and he was ecstatic. Taking Elaine and Nick by the hand, Greg knelt with them in front of Rick and looked up in amazement at the smiling boy sitting on his father's lap, holding a half-eaten cookie.

Greg was never surprised by answered prayer, but its realization was always an awe-inspiring moment, a heart-birth that raised everyone to a new level of existence. He understood the Kingdom of God would finally become visible, not by answered prayer, but by its recognition; that a unified cheer would reach a critical pitch that would shatter the veil between the visible and the invisible, just as the veil in the sanctuary had been rent with Jesus' final fiat at the moment of His death. *Into your hands, Abba ...*

"Okay, chief," Greg said to Rick, "put the cookie down and fill us in."

Rick took another bite of his cookie ... and moved his leg. An excited gasp escaped from the lips of his father who, up to this moment, had not experienced any movement.

"Rick! Rick! Rick!" he exclaimed, hugging his son tighter, laughing and crying at the same time. "Good boy, son! Do it again!"

Dr. Stephen Matthews and his wife, Pamela walked through the door in time to see Rick flex his foot and try to straighten it out from its turned-in position. "Ouch!" he cried out.

"It's okay, my boy. Take it easy. It's going to hurt because your muscles are weak. But don't worry, we will grow them back in no time," Dr. Matthews said, reaching in and grabbing Rick's legs.

Rick tightened his calf muscles and picked up his cookie again.

Greg laughed and said, "Come on, Rick! I'm giving you permission to speak with your mouth full. We're dying here!"

Rick, the expression on his face brighter than they had seen in a long time, finally focused his attention on those gathered around him, and said, "I danced on Gilead today, and when I came back my legs were tingling. It tickled, but it didn't hurt. The lady who sings to me told me to stay calm and wait until I came home to tell you. But Nick already figured it out."

Greg asked him, awe evident in his voice, "When did you go up the mountain, Rick? Who took you there?"

Rick answered, "I didn't really go up the mountain, and no one took me there. It happened when we went to the meeting hall after the rally. I just found myself there while I sat on Nick's lap. It was kind of like a dream. There were angels dancing and three boys were there, too. I met one who was my age. And there was a Man who was made of light, and everything was light because of him. After we stopped dancing, the man told us a story about a group of Indians who lived there a long time ago and made the mountain holy. They hid a manuscript somewhere up there that told how they came there to live in peace. Then he prayed over us and when he made the Sign of the Cross on my forehead, my legs began to tingle."

****

A stunned silence filled the room as the meaning of Rick's words expanded their minds and hearts to a new awareness, just as a baby chick hatches out of the darkness of its own small world and awakens to a new universe. They prayed together gratitude. No words were necessary or even possible. With their heads bowed, they gathered close and put their arms around each other, reveling in the awareness of the Divine Encounter, basking in the experience of a Love so deep that they were lifted out of themselves, raised above the ordinary, unencumbered, called to join the celestial choir, praising the Alpha and the Omega.

And suddenly they became aware of One in their midst 'like a Son of Man, clothed with a long robe and with a golden girdle round His breast; His head and His hair were white as white wool, white as snow; His eyes were like a flame of fire, His feet were like burnished bronze, refined as in a furnace, and His voice was like the sound of many waters; in His right hand He held seven stars, from His mouth issued a sharp two-edged sword, and His face was like the sun shining in full strength' (Rev 1: 12 – 16).

And He said to them, "Know that My Kingdom is among you, within you and without. You cannot go anywhere I AM not, because I AM. I have called you by name, to make the Kingdom known and in your humility, you have done that. Your patient endurance and longsuffering have not gone unnoticed and it is great pleasure to bring healing in your midst, for healing always touches more than the one and is ever expansive. Continue

151

your work of making My Love known. And know that I AM with you always."

And He disappeared from their sight, but not His Love. An even though they returned to their selves, they were touched and bounded by the Divine Encounter and would never be the same.

****

Rick put his cookie down, put his hands on each side of his mother's face, and said, "The cookies have cooled off, Mom."

Everyone laughed and Elaine said, "I guess I'll just have to get busy making another batch. Even more, I invite all of you to stay and celebrate with us over dinner. Can you all stay?"

Dr. Matthews said, "Pamela and I would be honored to be part of this celebration."

And Pamela added, "Let's prepare this feast together, Elaine."

Brian hugged his wife, and said, "That sounds like a plan to me, Elaine. I'll have to drag myself back out to the field to finish what I was doing. That's not going to be too easy right now."

Nick said, "I'll help, dad. Then we can get done faster."

Greg walked to the door. "You can count on my help too, Brian, especially if I get a ride on the tractor."

As Greg, Brian, and Nick went out the back door, Brian slapped Greg on the back and could be heard

saying, "Maybe I can hook up a plow to the back of your motorcycle. Now that would be a sight!"

It had been the best day ever.

CHAPTER 9

Sleepless Dreaming

As the first faint rays of sunlight pierced the darkness, Matthew knew it was time to compose himself. He had spent a restless night, tossing and turning, trying to find a cool spot for his feet, his pillow soaked from tears and sweat. In the darkness, grief had descended on him like the crash landing of a Boeing 747and had him pinned to the floor.

He had tried to lie still in bed and figure things out. He didn't want to disturb his brothers but that had proven impossible. Spying the large, smiling teddy bear sitting on the floor, Matthew had gently lifted it and tucked it in next to James as he slid out of bed, grabbing his pillow on the way. There on the floor grief pounced upon him like an avalanche, as he buried his face in his pillow to stifle his sobs. He had given himself over to the joviality of the day and had enjoyed himself, but deep inside, he knew everything had just been a reminder of what he lost, family, friends, church … home. Everything that had provided him with a life of comfort and security was behind him now. And as wonderful as Sam and Martha were, there was no hint of permanence for them here. They were three lost boys on a journey somewhere and they didn't even have a map. Fear had a chokehold around his heart and he began to despair. *Where was God? Were they just living a lie, believing they were being helped, were being guided? Their plan seemed so silly now. Why did their parents have to die?*

'Mommy!' Matthew sobbed into his pillow. *'Mommy, I miss you so much! I am so scared! Everything is soooo dark! What do we do now? Mama! I want to come home!"*

Sobs racked his body and he tried to quell them. He had to try to regain control of his grief, so he could be of use to his brothers. No matter how bad he felt he couldn't let Joseph and James down ... his beautiful brothers. At least they were still together. Thank God! And their plan wasn't all that silly. They had been able to come up with it in their panic ... together, hadn't they? And they had prayed first ... where two or three are gathered ... thank you, Abba ... please hug Mom for me. Exhaustion finally gave way to a restless slumber.

****

In the darkness, Joseph had lain perfectly still, hardly daring to breathe, waiting for the right moment to reach out to Matthew. As soon as he was certain that Matthew was asleep, he slinked out of bed and tiptoed around. Reaching for the afghan that was draped over the back of a rocking chair, he covered his brother and tiptoed back to bed, slipping into his jeans and tee shirt before climbing back under the covers ... just in case.

****

A heavenly glow caressed the darkness then and the darkness could not overcome it. Magnificent white beings filled the room and from their midst came forth one who had been called Mom by Joseph, Matthew, and James.

156

She hovered over Matthew, enveloping him in warmth, peace, and love, and whispered into his dream, 'I am with you, son. I am with you always. Never fear or forget what I taught you. You are always touching heaven, you just cannot see it. You and your brothers are forever in my and your father's embrace. You are on a very sacred journey. Trust Abba to place the right people on your path. Stay alert. Keep up your courage and hard work. I am very proud of you.'

Matthew's sobs subsided as his mother covered his face with her kisses, then she moved over to Joseph and James and caressed them, covering their faces with her kisses, and whispering her love for them in their dreams. She remained with them a while longer, bringing to their dream stories of the good times they had shared, singing to them the lullabies of their infancy, reminding them of God's love and of eternity ... encouraging them to follow their hearts for God was leading them home ... together.

The host of angels circled the room, their melody and praise rising and mixing with the incense of the heavens and the fervent prayer of a mother for her three sons. She could no longer feel sadness or cry for there was no pain or grief in the realm where she now dwelt with God, who would respond to her intense plea for her sons ... and for a place they could call home. Her prayer was also full of gratitude to Mary and Jesus who had reassured her as she lay dying at the scene of the accident. What appeared to the world as a tragedy would work out for good because they were beloved of God and because they loved him. At the moment their parents had crossed over, Abba had commanded an angel sentry to surround the boys, to help them carry their burden, for their grief would be difficult to bear, their love for each other so profound.

She leaned over each son once more, kissing them ... lingering a while longer over Matthew for his breathing was still ragged, his shoulders trembling from the force of his grief. He was sleeping now, and the dream she had breathed into him would provide some measure of consolation.

Her mission accomplished, the mother summoned the angels to escort her back behind the veil. And as the glow of her visit faded, she thanked Martha for inviting her in.

****

As the first faint rays of the sun began to pierce the darkness, Rocco sat up and stared hard into the darkness, searching for her. Sleep had eluded him all night and he had tried his hardest to seize her. Each time she had come within a hairsbreadth of his grasp, taunting him, *'Here I am, Rocco, come and get me'* ... and then she would laugh and dart away ... and he would continue the chase, because he needed her. Dear God, he needed her. *'Don't let me push her away this time. Don't let me lose her again. Please, Lord, don't let me play the fool again.'* Then Teresa would stop running and turn to him, her arms outstretched, her eyes pleading, *'Come to me, Rocco. I need you, too.'*

And when his thrashing about awakened him, she was gone, vanished into the darkness. He must have been dreaming, must have somehow been able to pounce

158

on sleep, and had landed on the floor, on his face, in a pool of sweat and tears.

'Pull yourself together, Rocco. Get a grip. Uncle Jake is going to think there's a war going on in here.'

****

In the next room, Jake did indeed think there was a war going on, and he knew why. Teresa was back and Rocco had to face it again, his feelings for her and the real reason he always pushed her away. And Teresa had obliged him each time. But the confusion and hurt in her eyes that she kept hidden behind ready smiles, cheerful humor, and traveling had not gone unnoticed by Jake. He knew that the reason Teresa enjoyed life on wheels was that she was really running away from home … Rocco … they were the same. They were in love, always had been, and they needed to be together. How Jake wished he could soften their pain, shove them in the right direction, but he knew he couldn't interfere. He had to remain silent on the sidelines, and wait to be invited. But he could pray, and that he did with every fiber of his being. And he knew Mary Anne was praying as well. This time would be the charm. He could feel it in his bones.

****

Rocco headed toward the bathroom to splash cold water on his face, not to wash the sleep away by any means, but to try to clear away the evidence of his battle.

159

Good thing Uncle Jake couldn't look on the inside, although sometimes Rocco felt that he could. No secret remained hidden for Rocco felt his uncle could see deep into his soul. Satisfied that he had done his best, Rocco headed back to his room to get dressed. The sight that met his eyes both stunned and amused him. He certainly had fought a war on the bed ... and off it. The bed wasn't just messed up, it was dismantled. He'd have to put the room back in order before his uncle woke, if he wasn't awake already. How would he explain himself? He'd had a fun day and just couldn't settle down? That would be like trying to ignore the sunshine coming through a picture window. Or he could say he was excited about being on the new school committee ... with Teresa. Yeah, right. His uncle would see through that one before he got the whole sentence out, and then they'd both be rolling on the floor in a fit of laughter. Maybe this time he would finally have to face his nightmare head on ... and survive. And Uncle Jake would help him, was in fact waiting to be asked, Rocco knew. His wonderful uncle had always been there for him ... had been there without ever prying, but always building him up, trying to make him feel like somebody. By now, everything was back in place, the mattress, sheets, blankets, himself ... on the outside, at least ... and at most.

Rocco tiptoed past his uncle's room, heading to the kitchen, hoping to make the coffee and have the first cup alone. He needed more time to think ... or not. Like the grand finale of a fireworks display invading the dark of night, Rocco heard the loud, rapid gurgling of the coffeemaker displace the silence of the new day as the last drips of coffee filled the carafe.

160

Uncle Jake was already sitting at the kitchen table, sipping his coffee and reading the newspaper when Rocco entered. Observing that his place already was set with a fresh cup of coffee and the sports section next to it, Rocco took his seat, keeping his head down. His uncle must have heard him coming. The irony of tiptoeing away from a war zone struck his funny bone, and he couldn't stifle a chuckle.

"I'm sorry if I woke you up too early, Uncle Jake. Thanks for making the coffee."

Jake tried to keep a straight face, but he couldn't keep the smile out of his eyes.

"My pleasure, Rocco. Thank you for staying over again last night. It's always nice to have the company of my favorite nephew." Jake cleared his throat and continued, "By the way, who won?"

Rocco glanced up at his uncle and they burst out laughing. The knee-slapping hilarity continued as they both doubled over laughing and snorting. When the tension of humor and grief had been relieved, Rocco looked into his coffee mug, and said, "I hope I didn't keep you awake all night, Uncle Jake. I'm awfully sorry if I did. I know we have a busy day ahead of us."

"It's okay, Rocco. I wouldn't have missed it for the world. And you still didn't answer my question."

"Nobody won yet, Jake. It's a work in progress."

Jake put down the newspaper and folded his hands around his coffee mug. "Talk to me, son. My ears and shoulders are open. Saying things out loud takes the fear out. And don't worry about a busy day. That's why we

161

opened for a few hours yesterday, so we wouldn't be overwhelmed today. Thanks to you, our work is already half done. Now speak."

Rocco took a large swallow of his coffee, and for a moment, paused to savor its freshly brewed flavor and warmth, the first sip that would rouse him to full wakefulness and push the night back to where it belonged. But he only got it half right. He was awake, all right, completely awake, but still staring face to face with the terrors of the night … and Teresa. And turning his head didn't change the scene going through his mind. His secret moved in perfect synchrony with every attempt to flee, like a perfect dance partner. *Why had he invited Teresa to stay for the summer, practically begged her?* His heart had spoken before his mind had had a chance to tell him to shut up.

"Jake, what was I thinking of, inviting Teresa to stay, like that? I'm only going to end up hurting her again."

"Rocco, I think you know the answer to that question. Maybe the time is finally right for you to say it out loud and face it. And know you won't be facing it alone."

"You're right. I think it's now or never. I do love her, but…"

"But nothing, Rocco. You love her. You know it. EVERYONE knows it. And Teresa knows it. She's back in your life for the same reason. She's here for you. Go for it, son."

"But, how can I tell her … after all these years? What is she going to think of me? At least now we have our friendship. I don't know if I can stand losing her again."

Rocco's voice choked. He stopped talking and stared into his coffee mug.

Jake reached across the table and put a hand on Rocco's shoulder.

"But nothing. It's just as obvious that she loves you. Go to her. You'll never have any peace until you do, and I believe you'll both come out winners."

****

Matthew fumbled in the darkness for his clothes and put them on. Picking up his sneakers by the laces with his teeth, he crawled around the bed and paused for a moment, listening for the sounds of his brothers sleeping. Satisfied that he could get away undetected, he crawled to the door but was disappointed to see that it was shut tight.

He had made sure that he was the last one in the room so he could leave the door open just enough to escape without making a sound. Martha must have closed it when she peeked in at them before retiring herself. Now it loomed over him as an insurmountable barrier. He looked back at his brothers and saw no sign of movement then reached up, grasped the doorknob, and turned it. If the door hinges squeaked and he woke Joseph, he'd just tell him that he was going to the bathroom. And he'd get away with it if he wasn't dressed and crawling on the floor with his sneakers dangling from his teeth. It would be easier to rob a bank with a squirt gun. But there was no squeak. The soft click was barely audible. Matthew looked back at the bed. He was good to go. Opening the door just wide enough to fit through, he darted to freedom. Now he only had to get past Moses.

****

One eye opened in the darkness. Joseph sensed movement in the room and heard the click of the doorknob. He had become concerned about Matthew during their fireside chat with Sam and Martha after dinner. His brother had been unusually quiet, deep in thought, and Joseph knew he was forming a plan, turning one over in his mind. Instead of joining in the conversation, he had joined Moses on the floor, to 'keep him company' and sat, staring at the fire. Sam had tried to draw Matthew in to the conversation but he resisted. And now Joseph was worried. Whatever Matthew was up to, he wasn't going to let him go through it alone.

Joseph lifted up another large stuffed teddy bear, and tucked it in next to James, as he slid out of bed. He grabbed his sneakers and blazed the same trail as Matthew and caught up to him as he slipped out the back door.

"Where are we going, brother?"

Matthew turned with a start, and gasped, "I thought you were sound asleep, Joe."

"We're a team, Matt. If you can't sleep, I can't sleep. So where are we going?"

"I have to go alone, Joe. One of us has to stay with James."

"James is okay. He's safe with Martha. Right now, you're the one who can't be left alone. You're stuck with me, brother. And now, for the third time, where are we going?"

Matthew sat down on the top step of the deck and put on his sneakers. Joseph did the same.

"I'm going to church. I know where it is. We passed by it on the way to the bakery."

"Don't be silly, Matt. We can pray here. Did you pay any attention to Sam? We didn't commit any sin by missing Mass yesterday because we didn't have a choice. Our circumstances didn't permit it. God knows our hearts, and he knows that if we could have gone to Mass we would have, that we really wanted to."

"I know, Joe. But I still feel like a hypocrite. Did we really try our best to go church? How can we ask God to help us if we don't try our best?"

Joseph saw the tears form in Matthew's eyes and put an arm around his brother's shoulders. Matthew buried his face in his hands, softly sobbing.

"Come on, Matt, we'll go together. We'll break into church, have a heart to heart with God, and be back in bed before anyone knows we left. We'll be back before the birds start singing. We'll be back before the rooster croaks three times."

Matthew spoke into his hands, "CROWS, Joe, before the rooster CROWS. Read your Bible."

"When we move back home, Reverend Valente, you can read to us from the Bible every night ... and I'll even listen."

Joseph and Matthew stepped off the deck, moving toward the footbridge and the back entrance of the cabin colony.

CHAPTER 10

In Custody

As the first faint rays of the sun pierced the darkness, Father Luke poured himself a second cup of coffee and moved to his comfortable chair by the large picture window in the rectory library. The birds were already chirping their morning melodies. Chipmunks scurried across the lawn and chased each other in and around bushes. Blue jays and squirrels competed with each other for the unshelled peanuts that Father Luke had scattered on the path to the fountain. The crisp morning air carried the scent of flowers that could barely be seen in the scant light of early dawn. It was Luke's favorite time of day, serene and quiet, a thinking time. A subtle breeze coaxed the dawn to awaken to the brilliance of a new day.

Luke sat in his chair, his hands wrapped around his coffee mug, savoring its warmth and enjoying the view on the other side of the picture window. He tried to make sense of the dreams of the night before. He was pleased with himself that he had cleared his calendar for this day, one of the few he ever took off. The parish offices would be closed as well. He had no plans, except to have dinner with Maddie and John, and Maddie was cooking. He had planned well. After saying early morning Mass, he would be able to come back to this spot and just sit ... and think.

The dreams of the night before replayed through his mind. He had been a part of them, something that had never happened before. He had always been an observer, like watching a movie, and then not remembering it when he awakened. But not this time. This time, not only was he

167

a participant, the dreams were still before his eyes, his mind. And one dream followed another, or was it different scenes from one long dream? He had awakened many times during the night, another oddity for him, and had gone right back to sleep … to dream again.

Luke hoped that he would be able to celebrate Mass without appearing distracted or making any mistakes. His congregation would notice that right away and become concerned, and he didn't want to talk about it yet. He needed alone time to ponder it first.

The dreams … or dream … had been lifelike, as if recalling an event that had really happened, like yesterday's youth rally. If Luke believed in visions, that's what he would have called them. It's not that he didn't believe in them, or didn't believe people who claimed to have had them, but to him, there was always a logical explanation … an intense desire to make God visible.

Luke took a sip of his coffee and savored its warmth. He became aware that it had just been one dream, one long dream …

****

He had been standing in a large meadow, in the center of all the action, directing, like an orchestra leader, but not wearing a tuxedo. Instead he had been dressed more like a ... how could it be? The realization hit Luke like a lightning bolt, and he put his coffee down and buried his head in his hands. He could not see himself in such a role. He was happy with his life, fulfilled. He loved his flock, those entrusted to his care, and they loved him. He

168

considered himself privileged to be here with these wonderful people, in fact, thought of them as family. In the dream, however, his congregation had been much larger, following his every move and in the midst of the crowd there had been three boys running, panic-stricken, the same ones in the photograph that had been circulating around the village, two with red hair. They were running hand in hand, the little one in the middle trying his best to keep his legs under him. And Rocco was chasing them, calling them by name, "Joseph, Matthew, James! Time to come home!"

Then suddenly the scene had changed. Two of the brothers had been grabbed and forced into two different cars and were driven away. They screamed to the littlest boy, called James, to be brave. They would be back for him. James threw himself face down, pounding the ground and sobbing. Luke had never seen fear etched so sharply on a little boy's face. He tried to reach out to comfort him, but became aware of a presence standing with him, One like a Son of Man, telling him to wait, the time was not yet right, but soon would be. Luke looked again and saw Rick leaning over James. But Rick was different. He had braces on his leg and was leaning on crutches. Luke was surprised and delighted that Rick was finally getting stronger. He laid his crutches down, knelt next to James, and cradled his head in his lap for a few moments, stroking his head, and telling him it was going to be all right. Then Rick stood, pulling James up with him. Picking up his crutches, Rick took James toward a mountain, and they disappeared behind a grove of trees.

And Rocco was again running, but now, Teresa was chasing him, calling to him, 'please don't leave me again! I need you! Come back! Rocco, come home!' Rocco turned back and told Teresa, "I have to find our sons first. Did you see where they went?" The sound of thunder drowned out the rest of their conversation.

The One standing with Luke leaned toward him and placed a Bishop's mitre on his head and a shepherd's crook in his hand, and said, 'Feed my sheep, Luke.' Luke knelt on the ground, and bowing his head, said, 'Command your humble servant.' Raising him up, Jesus said, 'Bring my lambs home, Luke. Bring my lambs home."

"But I do not know how, Lord.''

"You will know when they come to you. And I will be with you, Luke, as I AM always with you, and you are always with me. Together we will build the Kingdom and bring healing to those of Wounded Heart. Feed my sheep."

"Yes, Lord."

And Luke turned and raised his staff and suddenly before him stood all the people of the village, and with him were religious leaders of all the congregations. In the midst of them, next to Luke, the One remained present, His hands raised in blessing. Kneeling at an altar with their heads bowed were a bride and groom. The groom was Rocco, but Luke could not see who the bride was. She was dressed in a flowing, white lace bridal gown with a train that reached to the edge of the meadow and seemed to go beyond. A veil covered her face, her delicate features barely discernible. The One turned to Luke, and said, '"their generous hearts will encompass all I send to them. Their union will provide a dwelling place for the uprooted and desperate. I AM responding to the pleas of those who gave them birth, and I will bless them through you. And their Love will transcend every boundary. Luke, tend my sheep.'

Just as Rocco, his eyes glistening, was about to lift his bride's veil, the ground shook beneath them and the sky grew ominous as hundreds of motorcycles raced across the meadow toward the mountain, the riders dressed all in black. Luke raced across the meadow shouting for Rick and James to hide, shouting for the gang to leave for they were on sacred ground. Maddie was running with him, telling him to be brave.

'Now is the time to make them leave, Luke. Don't show them you're scared.'

Luke's determination melted his fear. He saw that he was not alone, for all of the religious leaders were running with him and shouting for the gang to leave. And even more, Luke heard a great multitude behind him calling with one voice for the gang to leave, the whole village united, one mind, one heart, one purpose – everything for the Kingdom.

Suddenly the motorcycles turned and raced away, leaving town by the back roads. When Luke turned back to the altar, the wedding scene was gone. In its place a small white coffin, covered with red, yellow and violet roses, was poised over a freshly dug grave, about to be lowered. Kneeling on the ground with his forehead leaning on the coffin and sobbing was Greg. Luke walked over to him, and kneeling next to him, put his arm around him and said, 'He is not here, Greg. God has raised him to dwell with Him. He fulfilled his mission and God fulfilled His promise. He now wears a martyr's crown.'

Luke had awakened with a start and knew that any attempt to go back to sleep would be futile. He put on his robe and sat in his rocker, trying to make sense of the dream. Each time he had awakened and gone back to sleep, he had returned to the same dream. And, each time, it had progressed a step further. But the last part upset him up so much that he couldn't bring himself to close his eyes again. He remembered the whole event in vivid detail, except for the very last part. In the dream, he knew who was in the coffin, but upon awakening, it was the only detail that he could not recall. And he didn't want to go back and find out.

Luke shook himself out of his reverie and finished his coffee. He returned to his room and knelt by his bed to pray the Morning Office, then offered the dream up to God for understanding. Was God asking something of him? Is that why the dream merged with memory? This was a good one for Maddie. Maybe he would invite her to have lunch with him and talk it over.

****

The ringing of the telephone shook Mary Anne out of her reverie. Putting her coffee mug down, she reached for the phone, and answered, "Good morning, Landolfe Bakery."

"Good morning, Mom. When did the bakery move?"

172

"Very funny, Teresa. You belong on stage. By the way, thank you for checking in with me after you got home last night."

"You're welcome, Mom. I knew you wouldn't go to bed until I called. That means a lot to me."

"Thank you, sweetie. What's on your plate today? You sound like you're up and ready to run. Are my girls getting ready for school?"

"Yes, Mom. They're already dressed and eating their breakfast and watching their favorite cartoon. None of us could sleep too well last night. Jessica and Bernadette can't wait for the school year to end so they can spend the summer with their favorite Nana."

"And what about you, dear? Were you too 'excited' to sleep as well?"

"Oh, Mom."

"Spill, Teresa. You've never called on a Monday morning before, especially after we've checked in with each other the night before. Speak."

"I thought you knew everything."

"I know you need to talk, and I just happen to have two good ears."

"Thanks, Mom. I took a personal leave day today since my students aren't back from their trip yet. I thought I'd spend the day with you, if you have time."

"I always have time for you. Since it's Monday, we'll have the bakery to ourselves. It's the slowest day of the week. Are you okay to drive? I could close for the day and come over to your place."

"I'll be fine, Mom. The drive in will give me time to think. I'll bring the girls to school and see you in an hour," Teresa paused, then added, "Thanks, Mom."

"Thank you, honey. I'll be looking forward to spending another day with my favorite daughter."

After Teresa hung up, Mary Anne held the receiver against her chest, losing herself in thought. There had been a tremor in Teresa's voice and Mary Anne was sure what … or who … it was about. She had put on a good show the day before showing the same excitement as her daughters about staying for the summer, but Mary Anne noticed the knit brow, the faraway look … the stress lines across her forehead.

The rapid series of beeps coming from the receiver abruptly brought Mary Anne back to the present. Placing the phone back in its cradle, Mary Anne rose from her comfortable chair by the picture window and walked into the kitchen to get ready. She looked through the cupboard until she found the special coffee blend she had been saving for such an occasion. She opened the can of Deep Chocolate Bliss, prepared the basket and filled the reservoir with water. She knew the exact moment Teresa would arrive and wanted the aroma of her freshly brewed favorite to reach her nostrils before she walked through the door. Teresa needed to relax enough to be able to talk … and cry.

****

Joseph and Matthew reached the edge of the woods at the same spot they had dashed through only two days ago. Crouching behind the shrubs and peering through

174

the branches, Matthew signaled to Joseph that the coast was clear. They emerged and walked up the sidewalk.

"Walk, don't run, Matt," warned Joseph. "We don't want to draw attention to ourselves. And stay close to the woods in case we need to duck."

"Maybe you should stay here, Joe. If only one of us gets caught, the other one can go back and be with James. He'll be scared if he wakes up and we're not there."

"We'll sneak in together, brother. We need to look out for each other, and Martha will take care of James until we get back."

Matthew surveyed his surroundings, alert to every sound and movement. Their angel guard also encircled them, an invisible procession to guide them to their sacred destination, and ready to reach out in consolation in case their plan went awry. Shrinking close to the shadows in the semidarkness, they crossed the street toward Jake's Garage. Matthew glanced across the street at Mary Anne's bakery and remembered her kindness. Joseph looked back urging Matthew to keep moving. Speeding up, they reached the narrow walkway between the rectory and the church and darted up the path, hoping to find an unlocked back door.

****

Luke glanced out of his bedroom window in time to see two tall boys dash through the side entrance of the church. It was rare to see anyone going into church so early and even more unusual to see youths entering at such an hour. Despite the dim morning light, Luke recognized the boys from the photograph ... and his dream.

As he turned away from the window, he caught more movement out of the corner of his eye. Turning back, he saw Officer Ralph crouch close to the bushes behind the church. If the boys came out the same way, Ralph would be able to sneak up behind them, and block their escape. Luke hurried out of his room, down the back stairs, and paused to take a deep breath before opening the back door of the rectory. He wanted to appear calm to Ralph and get past him without delay so he could have a chance to speak to the boys before the police did. He knew that if Ralph was crouching by the back door, the boys had been spotted and there were more police officers hiding by the front doors. From their picture, the boys looked innocent and would not have a chance to escape.

Luke opened the door, stepped outside, and crossed the footpath to the church, pretending not to notice Officer Ralph. Once inside, he headed to the sacristy to turn on a few lights then walked out to the sanctuary, carrying the sacred vessels for morning Mass. Glancing up from the altar, he caught sight of the two boys crouched against the shadows and kneeling in a pew, their heads bowed. His heart went out to them and he remembered the part of his dream where they had been forced into two different vehicles and sped away. They had struggled ... cried out ... struggled to free themselves, but they were surrounded and pinned. One of the boys had screamed out to the boy who lay sobbing on the ground, "We'll come back for you, James! We'll be back! Be brave!"

Father Luke thought for a moment, and then quickly scribbled his name and telephone number on a piece of paper before stepping off the sanctuary. He wanted his approach to be casual, as if intending walking up the aisle. He noticed that they knelt very close together and kept their heads bowed. Luke stopped just short of their pew, sat down, and turned to face them. The creaking of the pew got their attention. Slinking back into the shadows, they looked like they wanted to dissolve into the wood, and again, Luke's heart went out to them. They appeared desperate.

Luke smiled at them, and said, "Good morning, boys. Welcome to Holy Spirit Church. My name is Father Luke."

Joseph and Matthew didn't answer but knelt straighter and looked at Luke.

Luke continued, "Can you tell me who you are, and what brings you to Hillcrest?"

Joseph responded, "My name is Joseph and this is my brother Matthew. You've probably heard about us by now."

Matthew looked up at Father Luke, and added, "We missed Mass yesterday, Father. We couldn't make it. Will you forgive us?"

Father Luke could see the tears form in his eyes, and he answered, "Yes, absolutely. Please bow your heads and we will pray for God's abundant grace." As Luke prayed the Prayer of Absolution over Joseph and Matthew, he noticed how reverently they prayed, bowing their heads and folding their hands just under their chin. *They've had a good upbringing, Lord. Who wouldn't take these boys in?*

177

At the end of the prayer Matthew said, "We have younger brother. His name is James."

Father Luke answered the silent question, "Your brother James is forgiven as well. I can tell by the way you boys prayed that you didn't intend to miss Mass. God knows your hearts and has already forgiven you. You are welcome here anytime."

Joseph said, "Thank you, Father Luke. I hope we can come back again. But now, we have to get back to our brother."

Luke smiled and handed them the slip of paper. "Always trust in God and do not lose hope, especially if circumstances don't appear to be in your favor. Sometimes a rocky road is part of God's plan. Here is my name and telephone number. Call me anytime, from anywhere. And reverse the charges."

"Thank you, Father, and thank you for praying over us," said Matthew, taking the slip of paper.

"You are most welcome. Do not lose heart. I will keep you boys in my prayer."

Joseph and Matthew stepped out of the pew and walked toward the door they had entered. Luke remained in place and watched them go. He could do nothing to stop the inevitable but he could be there to pick up the pieces. He hoped he would have the chance to get to know them better. The words of the dream ran through his mind then, "Bring my lambs home, Luke. Bring them home." Was God asking him to do something special? Were these boys the lambs he was supposed to bring home? Home where? Luke, again, buried his face in his hands and prayed for guidance.

'Dear God, I am all Yours. Please help me know what you are asking of me. My answer to you, as always, is yes.'

Crouched behind the church, Ralph saw the door open and two boys peer up and down the path before emerging. He remained where he was as he watched them walk away. When they were far enough along the path, he pulled out his radio and gave the signal to the policemen stationed out front. As he kept his position, two more men joined him in the rear.

****

Joseph signaled to Matthew that the coast was clear and they left the church, moving up the path toward the main road. It was much lighter than when they first arrived. The shadows would not hide them now. Alert to every sound and movement, they reached the front of the church just as two policemen stepped onto their path. Reacting quickly, they turned and ran back, but saw three more policemen coming toward them.

Officer Bill Bennett called out, "Stay where you are, boys. We just want to talk."

Matthew turned to Joseph, tears streaming down his face, and said, "Oh, Joe! I'm so sorry. This is all my fault."

Joseph answered, putting his hands on Matthew's shoulders and touching his forehead against Matthew's, "Nothing is your fault, Matt. We got in this together and we'll get out of it together. Do you understand? Don't push the panic button now. We're gonna be all right. Understand?"

Mathew closed his eyes and nodded.

****

Bill heard every word and struggled to keep himself together. Those were not the words of rebellious youth. Joseph and Matthew stayed where they were, their arms around each other, tears in their eyes and heads bowed. There was no foul language, no threats, no panic. These boys had not given up but had immediately turned to console each other.

Luke had opened the door and walked toward the group. Officer Ralph motioned him to pass through. He came and stood in front of Joseph and Matthew.

"How can I help you boys?"

Joseph answered, "Father, we come from Valley Falls and our parish is St. Gabriel's. Will you call our pastor, Father Paul, and tell him where we are?"

Luke nodded his assent, "I will do that immediately. Father Paul is a good friend of mine. What about James? Should I send for him?"

Joseph shook his head and lowered his voice, "Not now, Father. James is being cared for. But can we call you later if we need to?"

"You have my number. Remember what I told you. Call me for any reason. I'm here for you."

Luke reached out to Joseph and Matthew, blessing them, and making the Sign of the Cross on their foreheads.

"Do not lose hope. God brought you to us for a reason and he will see it through."

Then Luke turned and walked back to the rectory to call Father Paul, as Officer Bill Bennett approached them.

"Come to the station with me, boys, and let's get to know each other. Maybe we can make this situation look a little less bleak."

****

Teresa pulled into the driveway she had backed out of only a few hours before. It seemed like eons ago. How could she have agreed to spend the summer in Hillcrest ... with Rocco, her lifelong friend, brother ... nonsense. She loved him, always had, and this time she didn't think she'd be able to run away again. As she stepped out of her car, the aroma of her favorite brew filled her nostrils and she inhaled deeply. Maybe things weren't so bad after all. Her mother was ready for her. Maybe this time there'd be no need to run. The idea of teaching in Hillcrest tickled her somewhere deep inside, especially helping to develop a faith-based curriculum for a new school. Faith and education joining forces under the same roof, a classic idea but imperative in today's culture. Good-bye California, hello Hillcrest. She shook her head. World travel and constant moving had done nothing to remove her desire to settle down in Hillcrest ... with Rocco. Maybe there was a way to run away from Rocco without leaving Hillcrest.

She climbed the deck stairs and reached for the doorknob just as her mother pulled the door open. "Hello, Teresa. It's so good to see you again. Come in!"

"Hi, Mom. Thank you for freeing up your time for me."

Teresa stepped into the kitchen and again inhaled deeply.

"Chocolate. You sure know how to make a body feel welcome."

Mary Anne hugged Teresa. "You just sit yourself down and I'll pour."

Mary Anne opened the cupboard over the sink, took out her two largest mugs, and filled them, placing them on the table in the breakfast nook. They sat quietly for a few moments, then raised their mugs for their traditional salute and took a sip. After setting them back down, Mary Anne smiled, and said, "Okay, honey, spill."

Teresa's eyes widened at her in surprise. Mary Anne laughed, and added, "Not the coffee, dear, your guts. You need to talk and I just happen to be here."

"You always are, Mom, and I appreciate it. But I already know what you are going to say."

"Then carry on the conversation for both of us, and I'll jump in when you mess up."

Teresa gazed into her coffee mug for a few moments, trying to compose herself.

Seizing the opportunity, Mary Anne said, "Okay, I'll start. This is all about Rocco, isn't it?"

Teresa looked at her mother, her eyes filling with tears, "Oh, Mom! What was I thinking of, agreeing to stay in Hillcrest for the summer? I don't know if …"

The works halted in her throat and refused to go any further. Her mother reached over and cupped her face in both hands.

"You do know, honey. That's why you're upset. You were thinking of Jessica and Bernadette when you agreed to stay. You're unselfish like that. And now you have to face Rocco again. Grab the bull by the horns, Teresa, and make him dance. It's what you both need. You can do it. And there's nothing wrong with making the first move. Don't let Rocco get away this time. Now take another sip of your coffee before your tears make it taste too salty."

"Yes, Mom."

They sat together in silence basking in the moment. Then setting their mugs down at the same time, Mary Anne took Teresa's hands in hers, and said, "Let's offer this up to God. Let's bow our heads and ask Abba to provide."

Mother and daughter bowed their heads, and Mary Anne prayed, "Abba, I lift up to you Teresa and Rocco, two fine and beautiful people, made in your image and likeness. Bless them and guide them. Help them to know your will for their lives. Give them the grace they need to face their fears. And it would be just fine with me if facing their fears finally brought them together."

"Oh, Mom!"

"Say amen, honey."

"Amen."

****

"Lunch would be better for me, Maddie. I need more time to think."

"You think too much, Luke. We will start with breakfast and discuss into lunch if we need to. Aren't you simply delighted we took today off?"

Luke and Madeleine were talking at the back of church after Mass. Luke was amazed he'd been able to stay focused for his congregation, especially after meeting the boys he had dreamt about. Only Maddie wasn't fooled and she had him cornered.

"You're right, Maddie, as usual. I was looking forward to enjoying a day off and ending it with a wonderful dinner cooked by the best. But today's plans have already changed, and we may not have much time to talk. I called Father Paul from Valley Falls, as Joseph requested, and he's on his way. He'll be coming to the rectory first and then we'll go to the police station together. Will you join us?"

"I wouldn't miss it. Come on. Let's finish here quickly so we can have time to chat before he arrives."

"Great idea, Maddie. Thank you for understanding."

Madeleine walked over to the rectory to prepare a light breakfast while Luke closed the church doors and turned off the lights. Walking up the center aisle, he glanced at the tabernacle and felt the familiar tug calling him closer, indeed pulling him. His steps became lighter, as if barely skimming the carpet, and instead of leaving church, he climbed up the steps to the tabernacle. Kneeling on the top step, he bowed his head and folded his hands just under his chin, his eyes closed.

And Jesus was with him there, two intimate friends, enveloped in each other's presence, the Knowing and the known, comfortable in their love for each other, communing through the sacred gaze of their hearts, the invisible and the visible, belonging, no longer needing words, Abba's message engraved upon Luke's priestly heart, "HOME". Again, the dream came to life. He was in the meadow and three boys were running, a little one in the middle trying his best to keep his legs under him. 'They are lost, Luke. Bring them home.'

Gradually the dream faded and Luke remembered the two boys who had snuck into church to be close to God and to ask forgiveness for missing Mass. They risked the danger they were now in because they were concerned that they had offended God. And he had been privileged to bestow the Sacrament of Forgiveness upon them.

He again felt the weight of the miter upon his head and the crook in his hand. Impressed upon his heart were the words, 'My beloved Luke'.

When he came to, Maddie was kneeling beside him.

"Are you okay, dear brother? You have me worried."

"I'm fine, Maddie, just overwhelmed with the events of the morning and the dream I had last night. There has to be a connection between the two, and I just need time to turn it over in my mind. Joseph and Matthew are in trouble, but they are not troublemakers. I believe God inspired them to take the risk they did for a reason but they don't understand it. They were in my dream and now they are in custody. God is asking us to help them, but I'm not sure what to do yet. Let's go over to the rectory and put our heads together. Maybe, between the two of us, we will be able to come up with something."

"Come on, brother dear. We'll put our heads and our hearts together."

CHAPTER 11

Touching Prayer

Mary Anne was carrying a tray of freshly baked cinnamon rolls to the counter when she heard the door chimes signal the arrival of patrons. She put down the tray and greeted Jake and Rocco.

"Good morning, Mary Anne. The aroma of your delicious cinnamon rolls and freshly brewed coffee assailed our nostrils before we even pulled into the shop."

"Good morning, you two. Jake, have you been reading the dictionary?"

Rocco gave a nervous laugh and put his hand on his uncle's shoulder. "He had plenty of time to read last night, Mary Anne. Neither one of us could sleep much."

"I know why I couldn't sleep," said Jake chuckling, "Rocco fell off Cloud Nine. I'm surprised his crash landing didn't wake all of Hillcrest. You're up and about pretty early yerself, Mare. Good thing. We sure could use another breakfast."

"Well, your timing is perfect as usual. Help yourself to coffee." She put some cinnamon rolls on a plate and handed them to Rocco. "Be careful. They're still hot."

Rocco took the plate from her. "The best kind, Mare. Thank you for having them ready."

******

Teresa came out from the back carrying a tray of turnovers. Rocco almost dropped the plate of rolls when he saw her but hoped his recovery was smooth enough to escape notice … except for Jake's. Jake glanced at his nephew, a grin curling the corners of his mouth.

"Ggood mmorning, Tteresa," stuttered Rocco, "What a ppleasant surprise. I didn't expect tto see you today." He berated himself for stuttering. Why couldn't he be elegant and dignified, like Prince Charming? But Prince Charming probably didn't stutter … or blush. And he had that thing going on in the pit of his stomach. *'Dear God, please don't let me hurl now.'*

Teresa didn't seem to notice, or was she just being kind. She wiped her hands on a towel and greeted Rocco. "Greetings, Rocco. My students are not back from their class trip yet, so I came back to spend the day with Mom. It's good to see you again as well."

As Teresa put the towel back down on the counter, Rocco noticed that her hands were trembling. *'So, Teresa is just as nervous.'* The thought diminished his stress.

The bell on the bakery door chimed again, and Leo and Ralph entered. Mary Anne, grateful for the distraction, welcomed the two policemen.

"Good morning, Leo, Ralph. Are you in for the usual?"

"Not this time, Mary Anne. And we have an unusual request. I hope you can help us out and I'm sorry for the short notice. Do you have any hot cocoa ready?" Leo removed his hat, wiped his brow with his forearm and put it back on, slightly off-center; so unlike him. He never wore his hat inside a building.

Mary Anne took a closer look at them. Their appearance took her by surprise. Both men appeared disheveled. The sun had barely risen on a new morning and Leo and Ralph looked as if they'd already put in a full day.

"Not yet, Leo, but it's no trouble. I can whip some up right away. The coffee is ready, though. Help yourselves." She handed them each a mug.

"Thanks, Mare. Is there any chance that we could put an order in for a large thermos of coffee, one for hot cocoa, and a tray of cinnamon rolls to bring back to the station? Something unexpected came up and it would sure come in handy."

"It's no problem, Leo, no problem at all. You two relax and enjoy your coffee while Teresa and I fill your order. We'll be quick."

Teresa began placing cinnamon rolls in a large pastry box. "I'll take care of this, Mom. You go ahead and sit with Leo and Ralph."

She gave a grateful nod to her daughter and sat at the table. Jake walked to the coffeepot, filled a mug for Mary Anne, and brought it to her. Rocco pulled over a chair from another table, turned it backwards, and straddled it.

"Okay, boys, fill me in. You both look like you've just come off a battlefield," said Mary Anne.

Leo reached a hand up to scratch his head and knocked his hat to the floor. He gave her a sheepish grin as he leaned over to pick it up. "I'm so sorry, Mare. I can't believe I'm still wearing this."

"Don't fret. Just tell us what's going on."

"You're right about the battlefield. But it's the wackiest thing. We faced down the enemy and found them innocent and without weapons. We've just taken into custody two of the boys from the APB, and they're not what you'd expect, not exhibiting any of the aggressive behavior their foster mother described."

Rocco looked at him intently. "I dreamt about them last night. The two older ones had been caught and were upset. The little one was lying on the ground, crying. It must have been tough to bring them in."

Ralph answered, "Not at all, Rocco. They were real respectful but the only problem is they're not talking."

Leo continued, "They're just clinging to each other right now and struggling to maintain their self-control, but every once in a while they start trembling. Won't tell us where their little brother is. One keeps apologizing to the other. And he keeps telling him they'll work it out."

Ralph added, "They're desperate. They keep looking at the door as if daring themselves to make a break for it."

Rocco shifted in his seat. "Why did they run away?"

Mary Anne put down her mug. "And how did they ever end up in a foster home. They don't seem the type."

Ralph said, "That's the tough part. They're not a menace to anyone. They've committed no crime. They ended up in a foster home because they're orphans and they want to be together. CPS was unable to find any relative or family who could take all three boys, so they were going to be split up. Their parents died in a car accident about a year and a half ago."

Leo took a sip of his coffee and set the mug down. "I'm on their side on this one. It would be crime to split them up but no one would get arrested for that. By law, we have to contact the adoptive families. I'm afraid this is going to get ugly very fast."

Mary Anne asked, "Don't the boys have a say? What about their rights?"

"They can fight it in the courts, but that could a while and they still have to be placed somewhere. It's going to be impossible to find a family who will take them together, especially since two of them are teenagers. CPS gave this case more time than normal but it proved an impossible task."

Mary Anne remembered when they came into her bakery, "The day they arrived in Hillcrest, they stopped in here and I gave them some pastries and rolls as a welcoming gift. They were polite and I could tell that they were not used to being on their own. I would like to come to the station and chat with them. Maybe we can work something out."

Leo smiled for the first time since arriving at the bakery. "That would be great, Mare. You're the one who'll be able reduce their jitters, and maybe they'll even tell you where their little brother is."

Teresa finished filling the order and said to her mother, "That's a great idea, Mom. Go to the station with Leo and Ralph and I'll stay here and make a few phone calls. The crisis counselors in my school district have dealt with similar situations. There is a risk here of turning good boys into troubled youth if they don't receive the right intervention."

Rocco said, "I would like to go, too, and meet the boys I dreamt about."

Jake finished his coffee. "Sounds like a plan. I'll stay here with Teresa until you come back. Everyone in town knows where to find me when I'm not at the station."

Rocco helped Teresa pack the order, his awkwardness in her presence replaced with determination. He said to her, "Will you have time to have lunch with me today? There is something I'd like to discuss with you."

Teresa rinsed a dishrag and wiped the counter. "I'd like that too. The girls know I'll be home late today. My next door neighbor will be able to stay with them until I get home."

****

"You're so right, Luke," said Maddie, "this is no ordinary dream. And it's obvious, not only because of your ability to recall it in such vivid detail, but you're telling it as if you're remembering an event and not merely a dream. God definitely has a hand in this one. You've had an encounter."

"Well, I know I never left my bed last night," Luke took a sip of his coffee before continuing, "and some of it was bizarre, especially the part about Rocco chasing those boys and calling them sons. Rocco flees from the idea of marriage like water from a burst pipe. What connection could he ever have with those boys? He has never even met

192

them. And the small, white coffin could symbolize the death of a child. That scene occurred right after I chased the gang away. What could it all mean?"

Maddie couldn't let the opportunity pass. Covering her mouth with her hand to stifle a chuckle, she said, "It could mean, dear brother, that you've been reading the Bible too much."

"Maddie…"

"Listen to your heart, Luke. God is speaking to you. And whether we call it a dream or an encounter, it is a message from God, ripe with signs and symbols that only our hearts can grasp. Even in the parables, Jesus taught the people using signs and symbols, and I believe he did that because he knew it was the only way to reach people and make them understand."

"There was a small, white coffin, M …," said Luke, putting down his coffee mug and burying his face in his hands.

Maddie reached across the table and put her hands over her brother's.

"It could mean the death of a thing not necessarily a person, Luke. Maybe it stands for new life or transformation. Remember that the prophet Jonah received word from God that Nineveh was going to be destroyed because of the sins of the people, and when he preached that word, the king ordered everyone to repent in sackcloth and ashes. And Nineveh was saved. I'm sure no one went back to Jonah and asked, 'So, why are we still here?'

Luke looked up at his sister and smiled. "There you go again, Maddie, pulling the sun out of your back pocket."

Maddie laughed with him, and added, "Relax, my friend. You and God are in this together, always have been, just like Moses and God. Moses wasn't confident that he could carry out the mission God had for him but he did. God formed him for the task of freeing an enslaved people and he's been doing the same for you. You have been preparing for this moment all your life and will not be facing it alone. God will get a grip on your heartstrings, Luke, and play beautiful music, and you'll wonder where it came from."

Luke laughed again and grasped Maddie's hands. "The best gift I have ever received from God was you as my sister. Thank you, Maddie. Keep me in your prayers."

"You know I will."

Just then the doorbell rang and Luke jumped up to answer it.

"That'll be our friend Paul, from St. Gabriel's in Valley Falls," said Luke. He glanced at his watch, and added, "He's later than he thought he'd be, but I'm glad we had a chance to talk. I hope he was able to get in touch with the bishop. He said that he had an idea that may delay the adoption of those boys."

Luke and Maddie hurried to the door to greet Paul. Maddie offered him some refreshment, but he declined.

"I hope you will extend me a rain check on your kind hospitality. Right now I'm anxious to get over to the police station and see my boys. They must be frantic."

"You're right, Paul. When I last saw them they were panic-stricken, but the chief was trying to keep them calm. Did you get a hold of the bishop?"

"Yes, Luke. I filed a formal request to provide foster care until a better solution can be found or adopt them myself."

Sister Madeleine asked, "Was the bishop sitting down when you asked him?"

Father Paul laughed as he held the car door open for her. "I'm sure he was, but he also took my request in stride, almost as if he knew it was coming. He said that he'd get right on it and I know he's a man of his word."

****

Sheriff Al Benson escorted Mary Anne and Rocco into the Officer's Lounge. Joseph and Matthew sat together on a sofa in a room decorated with comfortable furniture, framed prints, knickknacks, and a fireplace. An Oriental rug covered the floor in the center of the room. Around the rug, the hardwood floor was polished to the peak of brilliance. A table in the center of the rug was covered with a floral tablecloth and set with the department's best china and silverware. On the table, Officers Leo and Ralph placed a tray of cinnamon rolls and filled mugs with coffee and hot cocoa.

"I'm so glad you came here, Mare, Rocco. Your presence here can only help. Maybe you two can find out where their little brother is. The only thing they'll tell me is that he's being taken care of. And see if you can get them

195

to eat something. I've never been in a room where teenagers and food don't connect. It's just not normal."

Rocco glanced over at Joseph and Matthew as Al spoke, and recognized the sorrow etched on their faces ... remembered his own grief at the death of his parents. But his path to adoption had been easy. Uncle Jake had always been there for him. These boys were desperate to stay together and he felt anger rekindle within himself at the solution about to be forced upon them. And stronger than anger was his determination. There had to be another solution. Within his heart, he heard the message, 'You are my hands and heart in the world. They just need to be loved."

He had been fortunate in his life. When the two people who loved him most in the world had died, Uncle Jake stepped in and filled the gap. He never had to face his grief alone. God had been good to him, and now, maybe there was a way he could show his gratitude. He knew Teresa was back in his life for a reason. Maybe this time it was meant to be. She had stuck by him, even when he pushed her away ... his lifelong friend ... his love.

Gratitude overwhelmed him. His shyness and awkwardness had never been an obstacle because of the beautiful people who had always been there for him ... especially Uncle Jake and Teresa. *'Thank you, Lord. How can I ever repay you?'*

Then he remembered his dream. These boys were running, terrified, and he had been running and calling to them, calling them to come home. *Was it possible?* Teresa came to his mind again ... faithful, loyal ... beautiful. He would have to talk to her without

196

hesitation. Time was not on their side now. He could hide his secret no longer. *'Holy Spirit, please give me the strength.'*

Mary Anne and Rocco walked over to the boys. Mary Anne greeted them. "Good morning, Joseph, Matthew. I was hoping I'd get the chance to meet you again. I'm sorry for the trouble here. This is my friend Rocco. Tell us how we can help."

Joseph and Matthew smiled in recognition and relaxed. Mary Anne continued, "We brought you some cinnamon rolls and hot cocoa. If you hurry over to the table, I think you'll find they're still warm."

Then looking at Al, she added, "By the way, Al, this breakfast is on the house."

Al said, "Thank you, Mary Anne. You're always such a dear."

Rocco pulled a chair near the boys and sat. "Mary Anne is right. We are here to help. Thirty years ago, I was in the same situation. All of us in this room will do what we can. Come to the table with me and let's chat. Maybe we can come up with a better plan."

Mary Anne reached for their hands and pulled them off their seats. "Come on, you two. Follow me."

Joseph and Matthew rose and walked to the table with Mary Anne and Rocco. Rocco took two cups filled with hot cocoa and placed them in front of them while Mary Anne put two large cinnamon rolls on plates and did the same. The rolls were still warm.

The angels gathered around them, infusing them with a sense of well-being and security, as they sat at the table and bowed their heads in prayer, their hands folded in their laps. And Jesus was seated at table with them, His hands raised in blessing. Joseph reached for a cinnamon roll, broke off a piece and handed it to Matthew. They were again transformed and the whole room about them shimmered. Suddenly they found themselves back on the mountain and Jesus was telling them not to fear, to keep their hope alive, 'do not panic, my friends, you are almost home.' And James was there with Rick in the midst of the white beings. As before, they swayed, and twirled, and danced in unencumbered freedom to a heavenly chorus beautiful beyond description. Again, they were lifted away from burden and care, Heaven's scent emanating through every pore of their being, filling them with hope and peace and joy ... and joy. 'Do not be disturbed, I AM with you always.'

Rocco was standing in their midst as well, and he knelt on the soft grass. Jesus raised him up and blessed him ... he who had been burdened ... and healed him, and said, 'you will transcend every obstacle and your willingness to do so will bring happiness and fulfillment to many.' And Rocco knew the mission and accepted his part, and full of gratitude, joined the dance.

After a while, the radiance dimmed, gradually and gently. The swirling dance of the angels slowed. The music faded. Joseph and Matthew each felt a firm grip on their shoulders shaking them to wakefulness, and heard a familiar voice speak, "Come on, sleepyheads, naptime is over. You have a story to tell."

Joseph and Matthew looked around, wide-eyed with anticipation.

"Father Paul. Father Paul," they cried, jumping out of their seats. "Father Paul. Father Paul." They grabbed their friend in a tight embrace, laughing and crying at the same time, releasing the tension that had built up since their capture, a cheerful and tearful reunion. Father Paul held them close, his bubbling laughter blending with theirs.

"It's good to see you again," he said. "You boys gave me such a fright. Everyone back home was worried."

Al gave the signal to clear the room. The police officers and Mary Anne quietly filed out of the room, except for Rocco, who looked back, hesitating. Al moved over to Rocco and whispered, "Just for now, Rocco. You'll have a chance to come back." He gently guided him out of the room.

****

As soon as the door was closed, Father Paul turned to the boys, and said, "I am working on a solution to this drama, but first tell me what you've been doing, and where is James?"

Joseph looked at Matthew, and answered, "James is being taken care of, Father. Someone is helping us."

Father Paul asked, "Can you tell me who that is?"

Matthew answered, "Not here, Father. This room may be bugged."

Father Paul smiled at them and put an arm around each boy. "Relax, Sherlock and Watson. The sheriff has assured me that our time here is private.

Everyone I've met here is concerned about your welfare. You couldn't have fled to a better place. Now sit down and talk and don't leave anything out."

****

In the reception area, Al turned to Mary Anne and Rocco and thanked them for coming. "I know you lightened their burden and I appreciate it. But I have to admit, I'm stymied. They certainly do present a much different image from the one painted of them by their foster mother. And you were right, Mary Anne. They've been nothing but polite and respectful, even to each other in spite of their trouble. There was no finger pointing, no blaming. They've pulled together like nothing I've seen in all my years on the force."

Mary Anne nodded. "I remember the first time I saw them peeking into the bakery window. I knew there was something special about them."

"It's really quite amusing when you come to think of it," Leo smirked. 'We've spent the greater part of forty-eight hours searching for these bad boys and we caught them sneaking into church."

"Yep, their innocence really knocked your socks off, Leo," said Ralph, chuckling.

"Ralph ..." said Bill, a warning tone in his voice.

"It's okay, Bill," said Leo, "Ralph is just kidding. He just has trouble knowing where to draw the line most of the time, and I would draw it for him, but he would just see it as a challenge." He laughed and ruffled

200

Ralph's hair. "But don't worry, Ralph, I'll be there for you."

Ralph bowed his head and laid his hand over his heart, and trying to keep his composure, said, "Thank you, Leo. You have no idea what that means to me."

Al walked over to his desk and sat in his chair. "Well, you are all welcome to wait around here and see the boys again. I am going to release them to Father Paul when he comes out. He said that he'll be staying in town to see this thing through."

Luke added, "I've invited Paul to stay at the rectory and the boys will be welcome there as well."

Rocco looked back toward the room, his fists and jaw clenched. "Where will they go after that? I mean, what is going to happen to them?"

"Those boys are in for a rough time," Al said. "I had to place a call to Child Protective Services in Valley Falls. Mr. Munson is contacting both adoptive families. One family is in Vermont and the other one is in Montana. He will inform us when he has gotten in touch with them."

"But can the boys be forced to go against their wills? They should have a choice." Rocco began pacing and ran his hand through is hair. "I mean, what if someone was willing to adopt all three of them? Wouldn't that take precedence?"

Al answered, "Well, Rocco, that would be the best case scenario. The boys do have a choice but Mr. Munson told me that their aunt and uncle in Montana have a young family and own a farm, and they really want to adopt Matthew. They are interested in getting an older boy who can help them with the farm work."

Again, Rocco felt anger roiling within, like lava rising from a volcano, and he slammed his fist down against a counter. The surprise evident on everyone's faces mirrored his own, and he said, "I'm sorry for the outburst, but this isn't right. Matthew isn't a piece of farm equipment. He is a human being and old enough to have a say in his own life."

Father Luke came over and put his hand on Rocco's shoulder. "We have a few days to figure things out, Rocco. Leo is right. We are all on the same side, including Father Paul. He told us on the way here that he called the bishop and put in a special request to adopt the boys himself." Then looking at Al, he continued, "Can we delay things? I know you have to follow the law."

Al's sly smile answered the question before he spoke a word, "You're right, Luke, I do, but I don't have to be too eager. You know how slow we countrified folk are in these backward hick towns."

Everyone laughed, and Rocco said, "Thanks, Al. I'm going to the station to work … and think. I always think better when I'm working. It'll also help pass the time until Teresa and I meet for lunch."

Mary Anne said to him, "Sounds to me like you've already been thinking, Rocco. Do you have any bright ideas?"

"I sure do and keeping myself busy will help me get through the next couple of hours."

"That won't be necessary. I'm going back with you right now to relieve Teresa and Jake. Then you and Teresa can have the rest of the morning together and enjoy lunch."

202

Al handed Leo the keys to his car. "Drive Mary Anne and Rocco back to the bakery please, Leo. I've just had a vision of Rocco running up the street with Mary Anne's legs flying out behind her. Make sure they reach their destination ... alive."

****

It didn't take Moses long to give up on the important job Martha had given him, and when she came to see what was taking so long, all she could do was stand at the foot of the bed and chuckle. Moses lifted his head, whimpered, and tucked himself back in next to James, who was sound asleep with his head tucked halfway under his pillow, his arms around Moses. On each side of them were two large stuffed bears ...

Martha had been sitting in her rocker in the darkness when Joseph and Matthew snuck out of the cabin. She tiptoed to peek in at James, had indeed stood next to him for some time, praying over him, asking Abba to be there and protect him. Last night, as they had all sat around the fire, she had watched James struggle to stay awake. He didn't want to miss anything, but stress and fear had taken its toll on his little body and Sam had carried him to bed and tucked him in. James had been asleep before his head hit the pillow.

Now Martha stood there admiring the undynamic duo ... James and man's best friend ... and decided that it was probably wiser to let them sleep. James had the most beatific smile on his face, either from the wonderful dream he was having or because he was tucked in next to Moses. Breakfast could wait. Martha knew that the longer James slept the less time he would have to fret when he found out his brothers were not there. She would just sit out on the porch and enjoy the scenery until James woke up. And Moses would let her know when that happened.

****

Mary Anne closed the door behind Teresa and Rocco and watched them walk up the street toward the train station, watched Rocco take Teresa's hand. She had expected them to walk toward the cabin grounds, but she didn't really care which direction they walked, as long as it was together.

****

From his shop, Jake watched Teresa and Rocco leave the bakery and offered up a silent prayer, *'Please, Father, let this time be right. Please give Rocco the strength to tell Teresa his whole story. And help her understand that Rocco always had her best interests at heart. Amen, Lord.'* Jake took off his baseball cap and knelt on one knee. Then he put his cap back on and returned to his work, sensing deep inside that his prayer had been heard and answered before he ever uttered a word.

****

Rocco led Teresa into church and guided her to a pew hidden in the shadows. Their privacy was assured. Rocco looked at Teresa and felt his confidence begin to ebb but remembered the runaway boys and knew it was now or never.

"Teresa," he began, "I am really looking forward to you spending summer in Hillcrest. I miss you when you're not here."

Teresa ran her fingers through her hair then folded her hands in her lap. "I miss you too, Rocco. We've had some great times together."

Rocco leaned forward, his elbows on his knees his chin resting against his folded hands. Teresa placed a hand on his shoulder. "Talk to me, Rocco. You have something on your mind."

Rocco lifted his head and just stared ahead for a few moments, recalling Jake's words, *'She loves you too, Rocco; you'll both come out winners.'*

Jake had never let him down.

He gazed into Teresa's eyes and taking her hands in his, Rocco made the biggest leap of his life. "Teresa, I love you. I always have." He paused for a moment and looked down. Then looking into her eyes again, he said, "Did you ever wonder why we never got together?"

"You mean that story we told everyone about how we were too much like brother and sister to ever get hitched?"

They both laughed nervously, and Rocco said, "Did you ever believe it?"

Teresa said, "I believed it as much as you did. I've always sensed there was something you couldn't tell me, but our friendship meant too much to me to pry it out of you. I didn't want to push you away. I couldn't bear the thought of losing you."

"You're so right, but I was the one who kept pushing you away and you always came back. Now I hope you won't hate me for waiting all these years to tell you the rest."

"I could never hate you, Rocco."

"Do you remember back when we were in high school and I was absent for a whole month?" Teresa nodded, and Rocco continued, "Well, I had come down with the flu. Fever and dehydration landed me in the hospital."

Teresa said, "I remember you almost didn't make it. I never prayed so hard."

Rocco said, "I'm sure that I survived because of all those prayers. But my doctor told me that I would probably never be able to father any children and I knew how much you wanted to raise a family. I couldn't burden you with my problem. One of the happiest days of my life was when you and Ben got married, knowing you would be able to fulfill your dreams. And he was good to you, wasn't he."

"Yes he was, Rocco. We had a very happy marriage and two beautiful daughters. Life was grand and I thank God for all of it. But I am sorry that you had to carry that burden alone all these years. We're friends, Rocco. I could never hate you. I love you too much for that. I always have." Teresa paused, and then added, "And, you know, it's not too late for us."

Rocco pressed her hands close to his heart and closed his eyes, savoring her last words. Then looking into her eyes, Rocco asked, "Teresa, will you marry me?"

Teresa closed her eyes and Rocco watched her tears carve a path down to their clasped hands. "Yes, Rocco, I will."

****

Deacon John Salerno was just in time to see Rocco and Teresa locked in tight embrace as he came through the sacristy door. He turned and burned a hasty retreat back to the rectory, almost covering the distance without his feet touching the ground.

CHAPTER 12

Responding To Grace

Dr. Matthews had cleared his morning schedule to meet with Rick and his parents at Hillcrest Memorial Hospital to conduct a battery of tests and to map out program of recovery. Recovery … a word that had remained at the top of a blank page in Rick's chart since the accident. He had never given up hope, and it was with great joy that he penned phase one of his strategy. The way he had explained Rick's paralysis to Elaine and Brian was that part of Rick was still in a coma, was still sleeping, it would just take a little longer to catch up with the rest of his body. It wasn't a passive hope either, but one filled with physical therapy, exercise, and prayer. He truly believed that Rick would walk again.

The reward of keeping hope alive was now tangible. Dr. Matthews was holding and guiding Rick as he took his first steps, his parents, with tears in their eyes, cheering him on. Progress was slow. A snail could beat him to the finish line. But that wasn't important, Rick would reach the finish line and that was all that mattered. Dr. Mathews admonished Rick to tell his brain to make his legs move, and move they did.

"Take your time, partner. Slow is fine, just as long as you get there. Savor the moment. Concentrate on what it's like to feel again. Enjoy feeling your feet and legs move, touching the floor. Think of it as yawning and stretching. You do that even before you get out of bed in the morning. Give your legs a chance to realize they're awake."

Rick looked up at Dr. Matthews and smiled; that same beautiful smile that had been the first clue to everyone that he was waking up from his coma, the smile that had lit up his face even before his eyes had opened.

"Okay, chief," said Rick. "You're the boss. Wow, I can't wait to show Nick."

"Remember not to overdo it, Rick," said Dr. Matthews, "or you'll get sore. Your muscles need time to grow back and get strong. Nick can help you with your exercises like he did before. And those stretches are the most important part of your recovery." And smiling mischievously, he bent over and whispered in his ear, "So you can do normal stuff like climb trees again, but don't tell your mother I said that, or she'll chase me up a tree."

Elaine laughed. "If Rick's going to be able to climb trees again, I'm not going to stand in his way."

"Glad to hear it, Elaine. In fact, I'll join him. Well, this is enough for today. Let's go to my office and write out a schedule of appointments for treatment. I'll also come by the house every Monday afternoon to check on his progress."

****

Nick left school and hopped on his bike as fast as his legs could carry him to meet the best part of his day ... Rick, a mobile Rick, maybe even a dancing Rick. Maybe he shouldn't get carried away ... maybe he should ... maybe that would get him home faster ... to Rick, and his moving legs. A half-day of school had never lasted so long. Nick commanded his bike to fly, and since that didn't

210

happen, he settled for pedaling as fast as he could, his legs a blur on the bicycle pedals.

There was another reason Nick was in such a hurry. Storm waters couldn't flow over rocks as fast as he was pedaling. Logan didn't know about today being a half-day of school, so he would still be planning to rendezvous at their regular time at Cabin 34. Nick had called an emergency meeting with Tony and Frank at the cabin right after school to plan how they were going to deal with Logan. He was hoping to be gone long before Logan showed up. None of the three wanted to become members of the Jaguars anymore and he knew Logan was not going to let them off the hook so easily. He recalled the stories of those who tried. *Could they be true? Or was Logan just trying to scare them.*

Nick prayed they wouldn't have to pay the ultimate price. Logan seemed to enjoy telling them stories about recruits who had met untimely deaths after making 'mistakes.' He pretended he was concerned about their welfare, as if he was their Big Daddy, promising protection … yeah, right …like a vulture waiting for its victim's last breath. Nick prayed in the silence of his heart, asking God to protect them and help them come up with a plan. And he sensed that God heard him. He felt lighter, as if being lifted and it tickled somewhere deep inside. He laughed and almost fell off his bike. And he managed to do it without losing any speed. Then Greg came to mind …

He sped up the driveway, dropped his bike at the bottom of the stairs, and raced into the house. Rick was sitting at the kitchen table eating lunch.

211

"Nick!" he said excitedly, his smile lighting up his whole face. "Nick, I walked today!"

"Good job, little pal," said Nick, kneeling on the floor next to Rick to check out his braces. "Mom, how did Dr. Matthews get these braces ready for Rick so fast? Does he have a magic wand?"

Elaine laughed. "He had them ready this morning, Nick. He never mentioned it, but he expected Rick to recover and had already been working on them. The shoe is both a walking shoe and an athletic shoe, and the bars and cuff that go up to his knee are adjustable, so as Rick grows they can be changed to accommodate him, and a new shoe can be inserted."

"Rick won't need that, Mom. He'll be walking without them before he has a chance to grow out of them. Right, partner?"

"You got it, partner," said Rick, giving Nick a high five. "You're the boss."

"Have a seat, Nick," said Elaine, "I made you a sandwich."

"Can I eat it later, Mom?" asked Nick. "I'm meeting with Tony and Frank up at the cabin. We have to come up with a plan for losing Logan. Can Rick come, too?"

"Yes, Rick can go with you, but carry him. Dr. Matthews wants him to be careful and not overdo it. And don't let him try to stand without his crutches yet."

"Yes, Mom. Thanks. We'll be home before dinner."

******

212

"Shouldn't Joe and Matt be back by now?" said James. Martha could tell that he was trying to keep the tremor out of his voice, trying to keep his confidence alive … trying not to ask too many times. At least it had been the first time in almost an hour, for James had just awakened from a nap.

Martha had spent the past hour sitting in her rocker reading Sacred Scripture and enjoying company of her youngest guest. After breakfast, James had spread out a blanket on the floor in front of the fireplace and called Moses to join him. Moses didn't need to be called twice, and soon, man and his best friend had gotten too comfortable and too warm to stay awake. James rose from the blanket and walked over to the back door to peek outside.

Martha rose and stood next to him. She put her arm around him. "I'm certain your brothers will be here soon." James smiled up at her and leaned against her. They stood there for a few moments looking through the window.

James looked up at her and asked, "Is it okay if I wait for my brothers outside?"

"That is a great idea, James. Go outside and enjoy the sunshine." Martha held the door open for him then nodded at Moses, giving an unspoken command. Moses rose and followed James, his new best friend.

Martha hummed a tune as she closed the door behind them. The melody reached the heart of Rick, who was taking his first steps. *'It is time. James needs you. He is on his way to Mount Gilead.'*

'I will go to him. It will be good to see my friend again. My legs are much stronger now. Did you see me walk? It was fun.'

'Yes, Rick. You did a beautiful job taking your first steps. Be patient with yourself, my friend. I am very proud of you.'

****

James stood at the edge of the stream skipping stones and watching the ripples fan out, disappointed that his brothers hadn't taken him with them. *Why did they leave him behind?* He had kept up so far and had tried his best to be helpful. In his heart he heard Sam speak, *'You are a brave lad, James the Great. Because you have remained behind, your brothers will be able to come back. This is a critical part of the mission. Thank you for doing your part.'*

James glanced up at the mountain, recalling the fun of the day before, remembering the story Sam had told them about the Native Indians who had settled on this land, blessing it forever. He felt a tug at his heart that drew him toward the mountain, an invisible, but gentle caress urging him forward. Sam's words came to his mind. *'Come up here and share my favorite place whenever you feel the need. My friends are always welcome here.'*

James walked to the edge of the footbridge and stopped, calling to mind the rushing water, and the thunderous noise it made as it raced over the rocks, threatening to pull the bridge along with it.

214

Moses, who had stayed by his side, pranced halfway across the bridge and sat down facing James, panting and wagging his tail. James squatted and stared into the brook. The sun was shining and the water was still, as was James, but the icy fingers of fear gripped his heart, creating a paralysis that rooted him to the spot.

Moses barked to get his attention, then jumped up and pranced around the bridge. Failing to rouse James, he came back and nudged him with his nose, pushing him over, and sat down next to him, panting and whimpering, nudging him to get up. James did get up then, laughing and petting Moses, who turned and ducked around behind him and came up under him. James gasped, falling over on top of Moses, who dashed across the bridge with James doing his best to hold on. Reaching the other side, Moses stopped abruptly, dumping him onto the grass.

****

Martha, still standing at the window, laughed with delight. It was obvious that Moses taken too many lessons from Sam. For a few moments, James and his new best friend laid on the rich grass recovering from their surprise journey. Then James rose and walked toward Mount Gilead. Moses was close on his heels. Watching them go on, Martha was grateful that James did not have to make the climb alone. She knew the climb up would take longer today than yesterday because they would plan and romp all the way to the top.

****

Father Paul parked his car in front of the rectory and stepped out just as Teresa and Rocco were leaving church. Rocco grabbed Teresa's hand and quickened their steps.

"That is Father Paul, the boys' pastor from Valley Falls. Joseph and Matthew must be with him. Let's stop over there. You have to meet them."

They reached the car as Father Luke and Sister Madeleine stepped out, followed by Joseph and Matthew.

Father Luke greeted them. "Hello, Rocco, Teresa. I didn't expect to see you two here. Have you gone for your walk yet?"

"I bet they did. Their faces glow like they've been out in the sun for hours. Have the two of you run into any burning bushes?" Sister Madeleine eyed them intently, a smile turning up the corners of her mouth.

Rocco put his arm around Teresa and informed the group. "We ended up going for a short walk, but short was all we needed."

Then turning to Teresa, he added, "Teresa, I would like you to meet Joseph and Matthew."

Teresa reached out her hand to shake theirs. "It is a pleasure to meet you both. Rocco has told me all about you."

Joseph and Matthew returned the gesture. Joseph said, "Thank you, ma'am. It's a privilege to meet you."

Rocco turned to Father Paul, "Teresa and I have an idea we'd like to discuss with you, but we have a couple of errands to run first."

216

"Take your time. The boys and I will be around for a few days. We'll be staying at the rectory catching up on old times. I'll be looking forward to hearing about your idea."

****

As Rocco and Teresa walked up the sidewalk toward the bakery, Deacon John came tearing out the front door of the rectory, stopping abruptly when he saw the group assembled on the sidewalk. But he couldn't hide his excitement.

"Luke, Maddie, I just saw Rocco and Teresa in church … HUGGING."

"And, I'll bet it was no ordinary hug," added Sister Madeleine, completing the thought his expression couldn't hide.

"No, it wasn't, Maddie! It was a genuine twosome hug," said John, trying to speak and breath at the same time. "They were locked tight!"

Luke chuckled, and said to Joseph and Matthew, "Let me introduce you to our normally reserved and quiet deacon-gone-wild, John Salerno."

Then turning to John, he continued, "Turn on the dimmer switch, dear friend, the light shining from your eyes is almost blinding us, I'd like you to meet Joseph and Matthew; and you remember Father Paul from Valley Falls."

John shook hands all around, and said, "Paul, it's great to see you again. It's been a long time."

"That it has, but we'll have plenty of time to catch up. We can start now. First we have to pick up James, and then decide where to go from there."

Father Luke clapped his hands together. "Great idea, Paul. Let's get going."

****

"The sun is shining brighter inside that jeep than outside of it," Jake said to Mary Anne, as they stood on the corner, watching Teresa and Rocco drive away.

"And I think we both know what their errand is," said Mary Anne. "I'm going to close early today so I can be ready for them when they come back. I'm glad business was quiet today. It won't take long to close up."

"Me neither, Mare. Now I'm even happier Rocco and I did some of today's work yesterday. You know how much I dislike opening on Sunday. It is the Lord's Day, after all."

Mary Anne put her hand on his shoulder, and said, "I bet it was all part of God's plan and I have a feeling that the best is yet to come. We won't want to miss any of it so let's get a wiggle on."

****

Rocco glanced in his rear view mirror as he pulled away from the curb and laughed. "I don't think we fooled anyone, Teresa. Uncle Jake and your mother are standing at the curb watching us. It's almost as if there was

218

a lighted billboard sign above our heads screaming the news."

"Rocco, you heard Maddie. Our heads glowed. We don't need a sign."

They both threw their heads back and laughed. "I hope Jessica and Bernadette are as happy as we are, Teresa. We are asking a lot of them."

"Don't worry, Rocco. They have always loved you. Whenever we got ready to come in on Saturdays, your name always came up first. Don't tell my mother that, though."

"Teresa, I'm so happy I could bust. I don't even think our wedding day can top this. Thank you, beautiful lady."

Rocco heard Teresa try to stifle her sniffles. He parked his jeep and turned off the ignition. He turned to her and saw the tears she was trying to hide. Gathering her into a tight embrace, he whispered into her ear, "I love you so much, Teresa. What did I ever do to deserve you? Who would have thought?"

"We've had some wonderful people praying for us, Rocco. If Uncle Jake prayed the way Mom did, there was no way we weren't both going to be so blessed."

Rocco kissed Teresa then, holding her tighter, running his fingers through her hair, cupping her head with his hand. Teresa eagerly returned his kiss, her arms locked tightly around him, melting into his embrace, their hearts beating in unison, their tears mingling, one love, one life, one purpose, one hunger …

"Oh, Teresa. I have waited so long. I never realized how much you really meant to me until you started

219

talking about moving to California. That would have been much more than I could bear."

"Oh, Rocco, I only entertained the idea because I didn't think we stood a chance of ever having a life together."

"A whole life with the woman I love. And a family, too. I never would have thought it possible for me. Don't pinch me now; I don't want to wake up."

Teresa couldn't suppress a chuckle. "If I don't pinch you now, we'll never get moving. Maybe I should drive."

"I have to drive, honey. I'm in no condition to sit still."

****

"I'm going to sit on the porch, Nick. It's nice outside."

"Wait for me. You can't go by yourself yet."

"I'll be okay, and besides, you're busy. Finish your meeting so we can leave before Logan gets here."

"You are more important to me than Logan, little brother. Wait for me. Tony, Frank, and I can take care of Logan."

Nick got up from his seat to help Rick. Tony and Frank, who couldn't contain their excitement over Rick's healing, quickly followed him. As Nick lifted Rick and helped him tuck his crutches under his arms, Tony and Frank stood in front encouraging him. "Come on, Rick. Good work, buddy. You look good on your feet."

Nick reminded him, "Be careful, little buddy. Don't overdo it. No setbacks. At the first sign of pain, I will carry you the rest of the way. I don't mind. Understand?"

"You got it, chief. You're the boss," said Rick, resting in the security of his big brother's care.

After Nick made sure Rick was comfortable on the front porch, he, Tony and Frank went back inside to resume their meeting. Nick took a seat by a window that permitted him to keep an eye on Rick while attending to the business at hand. He refocused his attention in time to hear Tony say, "There's not a chance of Logan letting us go. And we're not going to be able to hide from him all summer."

Nick's eyes widened with excitement, "You may have just given us the answer, Tony. We'll drop out of school. Don't you remember Logan saying that they don't take dropouts?"

Frank said, "If my parents get a call from the principal, I'll be grounded all summer. I'd rather be dead."

"We could look for someone to beat up," Tony suggested. "Logan won't want to be seen with us anymore."

Nick said, "We'll get arrested this time for sure, and then get grounded all summer. Same as dead."

Frank had taken his pocketknife out and was carving his initials into the wood table. Tony leaned over to see what he was writing, while Nick looked out the window to check on Rick. The situation looked bleak for the three of them. At least Rick had fallen asleep. He was probably exhausted from all of the exercising he did that

221

morning. Then he had a thought as he heard Tony say, "Make sure you carve 'This is all that's left of poor Frank.'

"We could ask the police to help us. None of us has a record. We could tell them we were under pressure to join the gang."

Tony reminded him, "Logan will still come after us. The police won't be around us all the time. But it is the best idea so far, Nick. I think we're getting warmer."

Nick continued, "Maybe Logan will get arrested. After all, we are minors. Maybe that will get rid of him for good. We'll just tell the police that beating up those boys was a test we had to pass to get into the Jaguars."

****

Rick had indeed fallen asleep. Far from being tired, he had entertained the idea of taking a few steps on his own, while Nick was busy inside. He couldn't wait to stand up again, but then he heard the beautiful voice singing in his heart again.

"Rest, Rick. Don't do too much."

"James needs me. Do you know where he is?"

"Yes, Rick, I do. At the right time, you and James will be together. Enjoy your rest right now, my friend."

"I will rest for a little while. The warm sun feels good."

As Rick slept, the angelic white beings gathered around him, completely enveloping him within, suffusing him with Heaven's glow, lifting him beyond the visible, and

*carried him to the top of Mount Gilead, where James sat
beside Moses.*

****

James was beginning to panic. Joseph and
Matthew had been gone far too long. Leaning over, he
buried his face in Moses' fur and sobbed. Rick hobbled
over to James, stepping carefully over the grass, and leaned
over him.

"Hello, friend. You are not alone."

James lifted his head and looked up at Rick. "I
remember you. You are the boy who was here yesterday.
You came back."

"I wanted you to know that you are not alone.
I'm here."

"Have you seen my brothers?"

"No, I haven't but they will be back. I'm sure of
it. You'll see them when we go back to the cabin. First, I
need to rest.

"Before you sit, Rick, let me get a blanket for
you. Sam keeps one up here in the wall of the cave."

James rose, and Rick said, "I would like to see
the cave, too."

Together James, Rick, and Moses walked to the
cave, moving at Rick's pace. Upon entering the cave they
turned to the right, and James cautioned Rick, "Don't come
any closer yet. I have to stretch to reach the rock cover and
I don't want it to fall on you."

James stretched to reach the rock covering the
hole that Sam had carved into the face of the cave wall and

pried it loose. Then jumping up, he grasped it with both hands and pulled it off. Jumping up again, he reached in and tugged at the blanket, pulling it out. Rick had started laughing, and said, "I can't wait till I can do that again. It looks like fun."

James laughed too, as he bent over to pick up the blanket, but stopped when he heard Rick say, "I think you'll have to jump again, James. There is something else sticking out of the hole."

James looked up and saw what appeared to be a rolled up scroll. Jumping up, he grasped it and pulled it out.

"What is it, James?"

"It feels like soft leather, rolled up and tied with a leather lace. There's writing on it. Let's go back out and spread out the blanket. We can open it up and read it while you rest."

"I wonder if it's the manuscript that Deacon John was telling us about."

"If it is you can bring it to him, Rick. You saw it first."

"We'll hold onto it until we can both bring it to him. We found it together, my friend."

James patted Moses' head, and said, "You stay by Rick's side, while I run ahead and spread out the blanket." He picked up the blanket and dashed out of the cave to spread it out in the same place as the day before and then darted to the fruit trees to gather something to share with Rick. He laid the fruit in the middle of the blanket and ran back to Rick to help him the rest of the way. Together they sat. Both boys bowed their heads and prayed a prayer of gratitude.

Seated with them in spirit was another young boy, also six years old, looking for the place on the blanket that contained his sister's blood ... and finding it, he leaned over and kissed the spot, relishing the role he had played in saving her life, thanking God for healing Rosebud through him, thanking his brothers for choosing life over revenge. He heard his sixteen-year-old sister's laughter, melodious and angelic. He loved to hear her laugh ... and sing. Her singing had always made his spirit soar.

"Shooting Star, why do you always kiss that spot?" Rosebud asked him, laughing again. She already knew what her little brother was going to say, but never tired of hearing it.

"Because I love to remember what happened. My favorite part was when you opened your eyes. Your smile was more beautiful than a sunset."

"Thank you for being there for me, little brother. That was my favorite part, too, waking and seeing you."

Let me show you a trick, James. Then we won't have to loosen the leather lace," said Rick, reaching for the scroll. Inserting his fingers in the center, he closed the roll tighter and slid the leather lace off. Sitting side by side, both boys put their heads together as Rick unrolled the scroll to reveal a delicately thin, soft piece of beige leather, a hand-sewn border all around containing intricately formed script in dark purple ink written in the form of a letter. It was three feet in length and completely filled with writing on both sides. The salutation at the top began, 'On this shared day of the celebration of the birth of our Rosebud and our youngest son, Shooting Star, in the year of our Lord and Savior Jesus Christ, 1824...' Turning the scroll over and looking at the bottom, they saw that it was signed by Chief Lone Hawk.

James pointed at the signature. "The signature is different from the rest of the writing. Maybe their daughter, Rosebud wrote it."

Rick said, "That would make sense. The chief was probably too busy to write it himself. He would have spent most of his time hunting for food with the men of the tribe. I had to write a report for school about the Iroquois Indians."

"We did, too. I loved learning about them. It made me wish I could live like they did."

"Me too."

They sat in silence for a few moments, looking at the scroll. Then rolling it tightly, Rick slipped it back into its leather lace, and said to James, "We should go back down. Nick will be upset if he finds I'm not on the porch."

"That's a good idea. Maybe my brothers are back."

Rick heard his voice tremble as fear crept back in. He patted James' shoulder. "Don't worry, James. I have been praying for you and your brothers."

"Thank you, Rick." He helped Rick stand and put his crutches under his arms. "It must have been hard for you to come up here."

Rick answered, "It wasn't as hard as I thought it was going to be. God always provides."

****

Martha rose from her seat as the car carrying her new friends pulled up the driveway and ran to greet them even before the doors opened. Joseph and Matthew jumped out first, running to Martha as if it was something they had done all their lives. But, along with the joy of returning, she also heard their plea.

"Martha! Martha! We're back! Where is James?"

Martha grabbed them both in a huge hug. "James is fine, boys. You left him in good hands, you know."

Joseph looked at her sheepishly, and said, "We're sorry we snuck out like that. We thought we could break out and break back in before anyone knew we were gone."

Martha put a hand on each boy's face, and said, "Don't be sorry. Instead, see everything that happened as part of God's plan for you."

They hugged her and Matthew asked again, "So where is James?"

"He is enjoying this beautiful day with Moses. I saw them head toward the mountain. They must have decided to climb it."

Joseph laughed, "You mean to tell me that he walked across that footbridge? I would have paid money to see that."

Martha chuckled, "Well, not exactly, but that's a story James will have to tell himself. It was quite entertaining. And now, it looks to me like I have new friends to meet."

As Martha spoke, another vehicle pulled into the driveway. She clapped her hands in delight. "Wonderful! Sam is here, too. He must have been able to close his shop early today."

After all of the introductions had been made, Martha invited everyone in, but Joseph and Matthew asked permission to catch up with James.

"Permission granted," she said with a sparkle in her eyes, "on the condition that you come back as quickly as you can, no more detours. I've missed you too much already."

"Condition accepted, Captain Martha," they said, saluting her.

Sam's booming laughter could be heard as he closed the door of his jeep.

"My friends Joseph and Matthew learn fast. Now go find James and bring him back to the home front. I will be anxious to hear your stories."

Joseph and Matthew dashed off toward the footbridge and Mount Gilead as Martha gave a subtle nod to Sam, a plea from her heart, and held the door open for the rest to enter. Sam faded back and quietly followed Joseph and Matthew.